The Highland Clan
BOOK FIVE

# KEIRA MONTCLAIR

Cover Design  and Interior Format by The Killion Group, Inc.
http://www.thekilliongroupinc.com

# THE GRANTS AND RAMSAYS IN 1280S

## GRANTS

LAIRD ALEXANDER GRANT, and wife, MADDIE
John (Jake) and wife, Aline
James (Jamie)
Kyla
Connor
Elizabeth
Maeve

BRENNA GRANT and husband, QUADE RAMSAY
Torrian (Quade's son from first marriage) and wife, Heather-Nellie
and son
Lily and husband, Kyle-twin daughters
Bethia
Gregor
Jennet

ROBBIE GRANT and wife, CARALYN
Ashlyn (Caralyn's daughter from a previous relationship)
Gracie (Caralyn's daughter from a previous relationship)
Rodric (Roddy)
Padraig

BRODIE GRANT and wife, CELESTINA
Loki (adopted) and wife, Arabella-sons, Kenzie and Lucas
Braden
Catriona
Alison

JENNIE GRANT and husband, AEDAN CAMERON
Riley
Tara
Brin

## RAMSAYS

QUADE RAMSAY and wife, BRENNA GRANT (see above)

LOGAN RAMSAY and wife, GWYNETH
Molly (adopted)
Maggie (adopted)
Sorcha
Gavin
Brigid

MICHEIL RAMSAY and wife, DIANA
David
Daniel

AVELINA RAMSAY and DREW MENZIE
Elyse
Tad
Tomag
Maitland

# PROLOGUE

Ashlyn of the Grants sat in the solar twisting her skirts into fine knots, the fabric now drenched with sweat from her hands. Why had Uncle Alex, her chieftain, called her to his solar, a place normally reserved for the men of the clan? Of course, her mother Caralyn was also in the meeting, along with her stepsire Robbie, her cousins, Jamie and Jake, and Jake's best friend Magnus.

It had been a difficult time for all of them. Ranulf MacNiven, a man ordered to hang by the king, had been discovered alive not far from Grant land. He and another man, Hew Gordon, had joined forces with the intent of taking over the Highlands, beginning with the Grants. Then Gordon had made the crucial mistake of kidnapping Jake Grant's love, Aline, which had brought the might of the Grant warriors down upon Castle Dubh.

Aline had been rescued, Gordon was dead, but the elusive MacNiven was nowhere to be found. Ashlyn had gone with her uncle to the decrepit keep during the attack to ferret out information. They'd found more than expected, including hidden bairns, but two of the women MacNiven and Gordon had kidnapped were missing.

After all the abuses she and her mother had suffered before joining Clan Grant, Ashlyn was determined to help any woman used by a man. It had become her underlying motivation for all she did, giving her life meaning. Aye, she was a lass and not a normal Grant warrior, but she wished to show the world what she was capable of.

Alex started the discussion. "I've called this meeting because we need to decide how to proceed. Hew Gordon is dead, but we have no proof that Ranulf MacNiven is dead. He was not among the dead bodies as far as we could determine. I've also had several scouting groups in the Highlands, and we've turned up naught. I do not think he's dead, but we know not where he is."

"Mayhap he had another place to hide," Jamie suggested. "He'd only been with Gordon for a short time. There are a couple of moons between his supposed hanging and when he showed up in the Highlands. Where has he been? What did Uncle Logan think?"

Uncle Logan was not a true uncle, but the Ramsay and Grant clans were so tightly knit that all of the Grant children thought of him as one.

"Uncle Logan is returning to King Alexander to tell him that we have indeed seen MacNiven, and 'tis possible he is still alive." Alex steepled his fingers in front of his face, leaning back in his chair.

"Mayhap the king will have a suggestion on how he wishes to handle this," Jamie said.

Robbie said, "One other thing we can do is send a group of guards back every fortnight to see if anyone has returned to Castle Dubh. I would consider the possibility that he's hiding in a cave and plans to return to Castle Dubh once everything calms down."

Ashlyn spoke up, to everyone's surprise. "I think we should send out a search party. Search the entire area for unusual activity again, but wait until he thinks we've given up. I'd be happy to lead the search, my laird."

"Ashlyn!" Her mother jerked back in shock. "Why?"

Ashlyn reached over to squeeze her mother's hand. She understood the question, as her mother had not yet accepted her desire to be different, to be more daring than most.

Robbie and Magnus both responded in the same way. "Like hell!" The two of them looked at each other before turning their glares on Ashlyn. Her stepsire asked, "What the hell are you thinking?"

"I was in the kitchens, or have you forgotten? All that transpired there was not normal. Look at poor Aline. She was held against her will and beaten. Effie was held in the cellar with four bairns, and they were half starving when we found them. Cook said two other lasses who'd lived there had gone missing. Lorna was one, and Aline mentioned a lass named Cedrica. Neither of them have been discovered anywhere in the area. I do not like the feeling that was there. Something is going on, and I want to catch the bastard."

She and her cousin Jake, who had also been there that day, had reached the same conclusion. Something very strange had been going on at Castle Dubh. She reminded the crowd of some important facts they'd uncovered. "He did steal much of Hew's wealth. Aline said the two did not get along, but that the chief needed Gordon's money. Where was he getting it and why did MacNiven need it?"

Ashlyn looked at Uncle Alex, but the man who oft seemed to know everything did not have any answers. He merely shrugged, then said, "Logan also reminded me of one other important point. Do not forget what he said about Glenn of Buchan wanting revenge on us and heading to the Highlands, though he'd have a difficult time of it now that winter is almost upon us."

Jake stroked his jaw. "Aye, after they'd beaten me and said they were going to kill me, MacNiven had some of his men look at me to see if they recognized me. A couple of them said they'd just come to the Highlands, so could be they came from Buchan. One of them recognized our plaid. He said there were more men headed to Castle Dubh. What happened to them?"

Uncle Alex said, "Aye, I do not think we're done with MacNiven."

Robbie started to pace. "I must think about what you've said, Ashlyn. I know you're headstrong, but you're a lass. You cannot lead a group of warriors."

She bolted out of her seat and her hands went to her hips. "But I've practiced my bow and arrow just as Aunt Gwyneth has taught me. I had another session with Uncle Logan when he was here. Gavin and Gregor and I spent one whole afternoon shooting, and they both gave me pointers. I can take care of myself." Slud, how she hated the way men thought they were better than any woman out there, just because they were taller and stronger. Strength was not everything. Intelligence, cunning, and skill were oft more important. And Ashlyn felt an unquenchable need to prove it to everyone.

Her mother had advised her that it had always been the way of men, but she refused to accept it. The life they'd led before coming to the Highlands had taught Ashlyn that many men were dangerous fools. Aye, her stepsire and her uncles were good men—there were plenty of good men in Clan Grant—but her fractured memories of the time before still gave her nightmares. As often as not, she'd wake up screaming and thrashing, swinging at an unknown enemy.

Her mother was convinced her dreams were caused by a man they'd both known—Malcolm, the lout who had made her mama's life a living hell—but her mother was wrong. There were two different nightmares. One was about a predator she recalled all too well; the other was about a pair of attackers she did not recognize.

Whatever drove her did not matter. She'd practiced her bow and arrow every day for years. She deserved to go as much as any man did. And her heart longed to stop this abuser of women.

Robbie stared at his brother, his brow quirked as if he was asking for assistance in the matter. "Brother? Do you wish to send Ashlyn out leading a group of warriors?"

Ashlyn contained her impulsivity due to her respect for Robbie. He was the first man she had ever loved and trusted after the loss of her sire, and she knew he had her best interests at heart. Much as she wished to repay Robbie Grant for all he'd done for her family, she knew it was impossible. Though it went against her nature, she did her best never to argue with him. This would have to be an exception.

Alex sighed, pursing his lips in thought. After a pause, he said, "Ashlyn, 'twould be premature and rash to send you out now, especially since we've already scoured much of the area. I would propose we wait until Uncle Logan sends a messenger back with information from the king. If the king wants him caught, he may order us to go in search for him. If so, I'll send a group out."

Ashlyn managed to sit down and compose herself. "May I lead the group, if it happens?" She stared at her hands, awaiting her laird's response, not wanting to see her parents' looks of disapproval. Surely her uncle, who had worked with Aunt Gwyneth often over the years, knew how valuable a female warrior could be. Uncle Logan's wife was the most skilled archer in the Highlands, and many said in all of England.

"Nay."

Ashlyn jumped out of her seat. "Would you tell Aunt Gwyneth she could not lead a group? 'Tis not fair. You say that just because I'm a lass, Uncle Alex."

"Please sit down," Uncle Alex replied. "You're not going anywhere at present. Nay, I would not turn Aunt Gwyneth down because she's been trained to be a spy. You have not."

She fought the urge to cry, so she bit down on her lip hard enough to draw blood. Under no circumstances would she be caught crying in the laird's solar, especially not while discussing a mission. Her reputation was too important.

A few moments later, Uncle Alex added, "But I would allow you to travel with my warriors. I would send Magnus as your protector."

A smile crossed Ashlyn's face, but she felt it drop the next instant. Though she was grateful to be going, this was not a condition she'd expected, nor one she planned to accept.

"What? Why would I need a protector? I can take care of myself." Hell, the last thing she needed was a protector who might need to touch her, the one thing she could not tolerate from anyone but close family.

"Ashlyn, I have daughters. I know you think you can defend yourself, and mayhap you can at a distance, but when it comes to weight and muscle, you would not be able to protect yourself. If a man decided to lay you flat on the ground, climb on top of you, and rape you, you would not be able to fight him off on your own. Magnus would. I'm sorry if my talk shocks you, but you must be aware of what you may run into while traveling away from Grant land. Those would be my conditions. But we wait until we hear from Uncle Logan."

Robbie said, "Do not take it as an insult, Ashlyn. You'd be the first female to travel with the Grant warriors, just as Aunt Gwyneth travels with the Ramsay warriors."

Robbie had a point. No other female had ever traveled with the Grant warriors. She would be the first. Regardless of the conditions, she had been given her uncle's approval to help search out the bastard MacNiven. She'd find him for sure and put an arrow through his thick skin. If she had to have a protector, so be it. Magnus was better than many, though she'd never admit it to him.

This was what she'd always wanted.

She was now a Grant warrior. She smiled and nodded. "My thanks, Uncle Alex."

Then she glowered at Magnus, who had the audacity to grin back at her.

# CHAPTER ONE

*Early winter, The Highlands of Scotland*

Ashlyn of Grant nocked her arrow and mentally reminded herself of everything her aunt had taught her: correct stance, eyes on target, elbow even with her jaw line, allow the muscles in her back to take over. Before she finished her usual routine, a loud thwack sounded off to her left. The stray arrow had hit her target. She turned to investigate, but she appeared to be alone on the archery practice field. The men should all be in the lists at this hour. She knew Jake, Jamie, her stepsire Robbie, and Uncle Brodie would be working the men hard.

Ranulf MacNiven was likely still out there, after all, so it might not be long before their next battle.

She was about to return her attention to her practice when another arrow whistled past—this one far too close for comfort. She dropped to the ground, and the arrow struck the tree behind her. There was still no sign of an intruder. Was she the target?

She yelled out, "Stand tall like a man. Are you afraid of a lass like me? You dare not show your face?" If someone was shooting at her, then she needed to find out who—and preferably before the arrow embedded in her shoulder or somewhere worse.

Another arrow swished past her and buried itself into the tree directly behind her. Now she was angry.

She propelled herself to her feet, shouting, "You hide in the trees and try to shoot a lass? What kind of man does that? Who the hell are you?" Hellfire, she probably shouldn't be so bold, but she couldn't stop herself, hoping to catch the lout before he got away. Running in a crooked path instead of a straight one, she circled the periphery of the target area, wanting to shove her fist in the careless fool's face.

"Ashlyn!"

A booming voice rent the air and she spun around, only to see Magnus heading straight for her in a dead run. He was almost upon her when another sound distracted her. But before she could turn around and get a look at the archer, a huge arm wrapped around her middle, throwing her down to the ground.

Magnus. She shoved his arm away, but then grabbed him, tucking into his side, when two more arrows hit the trees not far from them.

"Have you no sense, lass? You're being shot at!" His arm, the size of an oak tree that had been around for centuries, held her fast to the ground.

As soon as her wits returned to her, she shoved against him. "Magnus!" she shouted, trying her best to disengage his enormous arm. It was fruitless, of course. There was more strength in his arm than there was in her entire body. "Get away. Leave me be. How dare you touch me!"

He sat up, releasing her as she swung her small fists at him. "Touch you! I was trying to protect you. Nay, I *did* protect you. Did you not see how close those arrows came to you?"

He stood and held his hand out to quiet her. "I heard something in the trees," he explained in an undertone. Searching the area, he held his sword out in front of him.

Her chest heaved, and she could hear her own breathing in the silence. Anyone would tell her that panic was a normal reaction to being shot at. But that wasn't why she was panting.

She did not like being touched by a man.

The lads in Clan Grant had, for the most part, learned to stay away from her. Magnus normally did, too, but she could tell he truly feared someone was after her.

Fear crept up her neck—the same prickly feeling she'd experienced so many years ago on a beach south of Ayr when she'd helplessly watched a Norseman beat her mother. She almost groaned because she did her best to bury those horrific memories, but they still found their way to the surface occasionally, especially in moments like this one.

As much as she hated to admit it, her fear stayed at bay because Magnus, one of the few men she trusted, stood in front of her. True, she trusted her laird and her cousins, but that was usually her limit.

Except for Magnus, and she did not understand why he was an exception.

After staring into the trees for a good long while, Magnus pivoted around to glare at her. "What in hellfire is wrong with you? How could you make yourself such a target to someone?"

"I do not think they were aiming to kill me, just frighten me. 'Tis just another daft fool who believes a woman cannot fire a bow. He's not the first to try to send me away from the archery field."

"Then if you are accustomed to such treatment, why did you not duck behind the trees to be safe? Where exactly were the arrows coming from?"

She settled her hands on her hips and leaned toward him. "How in hellfire would I know?"

Magnus leaned toward her. "Must you be so foul mouthed for a lass?"

"Why? Does it bother you?"

"Aye, it does."

"I'll speak however I choose. I see no reason you can say hellfire and I cannot. Accept me or leave me."

Magnus rolled his eyes and shook his head, letting loose a great, bellowing laugh. There was an edge of bitterness to it, she thought. "Unfortunately, I am now charged with your safety, so I cannot just leave you. And you'll do as I say because I'll not have you ruin my chances at becoming the future chief's second."

"You are not charged with my safety until we leave Grant land, so go back to your needlepoint, Magnus." She gave him her back and picked up the arrows not far away.

"Aye, I am charged with your safety from this day forward, so get used to having me by your side. MacNiven could find his way here. For all you know, he's in those trees aiming for your heart."

"Do as you must." Despite her dismissive tone, his words gave her pause. Could Magnus be correct? She'd assumed it was some lad trying to scare her away from the field, but what if it wasn't? What if someone truly had been aiming for her heart?

What a ridiculous suggestion. There was no one trying to kill her. Dismissing those thoughts, she turned around to glare at him again. "Just remember not to touch me. You have no right to touch me."

He chuckled. "Believe me, lass. We all know that touching you could cost us our ballocks. Do not make the mistake of kicking me there, or you'll pay for it. My only interest is in doing my job so I can be promoted. No lass can compare to my sweet Rhona."

Magnus made his way to the tree and pulled the remaining arrow out of it. "Whose arrow is this?"

Ashlyn calmed down. Aye, his Rhona had been a sweet lass, and the whole clan had mourned her and the son she had died trying to deliver. Mayhap the reason she trusted Magnus was because he'd always loved Rhona and would probably never be interested in another.

Finally a bit calmer, she turned the arrows over in her hand. "There is no doubt that it is a Grant arrow, but as I said, it probably belongs to a lad who was trying to scare me away. I do not scare so easily."

Magnus stared at her, his face only a short distance away. He smiled at her—that wide, white-toothed smile he was so known for—and his brown eyes might as well have reached over and stirred her insides. "Careless? Your innocence amuses me, but I cannot believe you are that naïve." Just as quickly, his smile disappeared. "Lass, someone was aiming for you. You must accept that their intent was more than to merely frighten you away."

"What? 'Tis foolish. Who would wish to injure me?"

Magnus was close enough for her to pick up his scent. She scowled, wondering why such a thing as the scent of a man would draw her attention. Neither of them was young and giddy. She was six and twenty, well past marrying age, and Magnus was nearing thirty. Why was she suddenly so aware of him? She scratched her head and tried to tidy her locks. What had they been discussing? Hellfire, but now the man was affecting her ability to think.

"Now, Ashlyn. Can you think of something that has happened recently that may have upset a young lad or two? A lad who works in the lists every day, a lad who desires to travel as a Grant warrior, who wishes to brag to all his friends that he is now a chosen one." He crossed his arms and stared at her, that pesky grin of his back.

"Must you always smile, Magnus?" she whispered, her brow raised.

He chuckled. "Aye, I must. Does it bother you?" His eyes widened, his face now radiant with delight.

She refused to give him the satisfaction. "Nay. Of course not. Smile in your sleep, if you wish." Then she returned her thoughts to what he had suggested. Could it be true? "My guess is that you believe someone is shooting at me because I have taken their spot in a warrior's journey. Surely, no one is that small. The men of the clan have been carrying out all the warriors' duties forever. Why would they be this upset that a lass has been included for a change?"

"Well now. Allow me to help you reason through this for a moment. Suppose you do such a great job that the chief decides to send more lasses on his next attacks or searches, not that I expect that to happen, but please consider the possibility for a moment."

"There are no more lasses who are interested in going." What a preposterous thought. "Where do you get such ideas?"

"Hmmm…and how would the warriors know that Gracie or Kyla or Aline wouldn't like to go along with you? You know how fast word travels, do you not? Do you know what is being said in the Ramsay clan now?"

"What?" Aline…hmm…she hadn't considered such a possibility. Gracie would never leave Grant land, and Kyla? She was more like her sire than her mother. Eliza, the youngest, was more like Aunt Maddie.

"Och, I see you have not heard that because of your aunt Gwyneth, her daughters Molly, Maggie, and Sorcha all wish to be trained as warriors."

"That's just silly. Molly and Sorcha are archers, true, but they have no desire to travel with the warriors. They prefer to travel with their mother and sire. And Maggie has never liked to leave Ramsay land."

She frowned, working this through in her mind. After all her hard work, she'd believed the other Grants would think her worthy of inclusion in the guards. But her stepsire had told her once that many men did not believe a woman should be fighting. Were they all so narrow-minded?"

"But…"

Magnus moved over to whisper in her ear. "Take my word for it. Whether you choose to believe me or not, there are several warriors who believe a lass belongs at home and not out with the guards. You need to decide how you'll deal with that on our wee trip. Because you will be forced to deal with it." He walked off back toward the keep, but spun around just as he reached his horse. "And you'll not be kicking me where you can hurt a man most."

She filed this in the back of her mind, deciding she should discuss the matter with her stepsire. If there was a special way of stopping a lad, she had best learn it.

A thought popped into her mind. "Where are you going?"

Magnus patted his horse before he turned back to her. "I'm going to see our laird."

"Why?" Fear rippled up her spine as his intent dawned on her. "You do not plan to bother him with news of this incident, do you?"

"For certes. Someone on Grant land shot at you. He needs to be aware of this right away, and though I deem it safe, I would suggest you leave the area with me."

She reached his side and grasped his upper arm. Magnus quirked his brow at her, but she did not flinch. "Please, Magnus. Do not tell our laird. If you do, he'll not allow me to go."

"Lass, 'tis his decision to make."

"But I've worked forever on my accuracy. I *deserve* this. Besides, you and I and Jake are the only ones who have particular knowledge of MacNiven. Jake cannot go, so I must. Please do not ruin this for me."

Magnus groaned. "My responsibility is to you and to our laird. Naught else. I must do as charged."

"Then tell Jake. He'll be the chief someday. Ask for his counsel, but please do not tell his sire."

Magnus mounted his horse, then turned the beast around to face her. "Aye, I'll agree to talk to Jake first, but if he chooses to go to his sire, I'll not try to stop him. I'll be watching as I'm charged to do, but you need to be more aware of your surroundings. Now, I'm not leaving until you get on your horse and follow me. You should not be out here alone."

Picking up a stick, she broke it and whipped it across the field before she climbed on her horse and followed him.

She'd show them. She'd show them all what a lass could do.

And they'd better keep their hands a good distance away from her.

# CHAPTER TWO

Magnus did his best to calm his beating heart as he rode across the meadow. He would not admit to anyone how affrighted he'd been to witness the attack on Ashlyn. Guilt washed over him, for he could no longer hide the truth from himself. He had feelings for the lass.

Aye, she'd been around Grant land for a long time, but he'd not noticed her much before. He'd only started paying attention to her over the last moon or so. She was a tough lass, strong and well-trained, and she'd done a fine job of helping Jake's new wife, Aline, escape from the keep where she'd been held prisoner by Ranulf MacNiven's partner.

But he felt guilty because of his love for his sweet wife. Och, how he'd loved her, but she'd left him near two years ago. True, she had not chosen to leave him, and many mothers die in childbirth, but why had the Lord taken his family from him?

Rhona hadn't been a strong lass like Ashlyn. She'd depended on him for everything. He suspected that's why he was drawn to Ashlyn. While he'd sworn to never marry again, suddenly the thought of another marriage was more appealing, and it had to do with an independent lass with lush brown eyes.

He found that independence enticing. Well, that and her luscious curves that were just right for his hands. She was a tall and voluptuous beauty. The complete opposite of petite, fair-haired Rhona. Ashlyn's hair was a sultry brown, rich because she allowed it to swing free most of the time instead of plaiting it. She did not go by customs.

He suspected Ashlyn would not have him, but a man could dream.

When they reached the stables, Ashlyn did not wait for him to help her dismount—she jumped down and hustled away before he could get close to her.

He shook his head. The lass was as prickly as a Scottish wildcat. Did she carry a wound from her past? Everyone knew Caralyn and her daughters had joined Clan Grant after escaping an evil man. Gracie had been too young to remember life before the Grant keep, but Ashlyn would remember.

Suddenly, he had a new purpose. He'd find out what was in her past if it took him ten moons. Mayhap he could help the lass if he knew what plagued her. He watched her as she strode away, her chin held high, ignoring all the men who cast her appreciative glances.

Jake strode toward him from the lists. "Magnus, did something happen with my cousin? Neither one of you looked verra pleased."

"Och, you know Ashlyn, she's a stubborn lass. There were stray arrows flying out at the archery field. She thinks it was naught. I believe she was the target. I refused to leave her out there alone, so she's a wee bit upset."

"Stray arrows? Who would fire at her? 'Tis serious if she truly is the target. I'm glad you did not leave her out there, regardless of her feelings."

"According to Ashlyn, it has happened before and she deems it due to some lads not liking her presence at the archery fields. I think it was more than that. The arrows were too close. I gave her something to think on."

"And what was that?" Jake's mouth curled up at the ends.

"I mentioned that some of the lads are upset about a lass traveling with the Grant warriors."

Jake jerked his head back. "You're lucky she did not take a swing at you."

"She did," he smirked, "but only because I grabbed her to throw her out of the path of the arrow. You know she does not like to be touched."

"Aye," Jake said, rubbing his chin. "We need to know what transpired at the field before we send her off to Edinburgh. Mayhap my sire will have an idea."

"She begged me not to tell your sire, only you."

"Why?" Jake crossed his arms as his gaze followed Ashlyn.

"She's afraid he will keep her home."

"If her life is in danger, she *should* stay here."

"But what if the person who's after her is here? She may be safer with us. Much as I dislike agreeing with the stubborn lass, I may have to this time." Magnus stared after her, watching the sway of her hips. Ashlyn did not have the teasing, saucy move to her deportment. Her demeanor carried a determined stride, a movement that demonstrated confidence in her abilities. He guessed her to be innocent in the ways of men and women, an innocence that enticed him even more.

"She's a stubborn lass, you have the right of it. I'll see what I can uncover, and I'll hold off on talking to my sire. His head has been paining him lately, so I'd prefer not to bother him unless absolutely necessary."

"My thanks."

"What do you suppose makes her wish to travel with the guards?" Jake asked.

"I suspect the same thing that is driving me—the desire to be the best she can be. She just happens to be different than most lasses. She wishes to ride with lads, and there are not many willing to do that."

"It's more than that. Ever since Ashlyn helped us rescue Aline and the other lasses from Castle Dubh, she has been determined to ride against Ranulf MacNiven. After all the fighting and death, you would think she would never wish to go back, but she's as driven as if she had a personal vendetta against him. Mayhap 'tis because two of the lasses from Castle Dubh are still missing? When they were wee lassies, Ashlyn and Gracie were stolen away from Caralyn."

"Has Aline told you anything?"

"Nay. She did not get along with the missing women, says they were both nasty, but she doesn't wish for any harm to come to them. For the most part, Aline would prefer to put it all behind her. She has no desire to chase after MacNiven. Yet I fear Ashlyn will not rest until she finds him." He stared after his cousin, his hands on his hips. "Do you think one of our own guards was shooting at her? Because if so, we must find and unmask the bastard before we decide who's going on the journey. He will be punished for his actions. You know how my sire is about men attacking women."

"You mean *if* we go. Logan Ramsay has not returned yet."

"He will. You can count on that. We've had dealings with MacNiven twice, once on Ramsay land, once here. He will not give up, and my sire and uncles will not let him go free. Neither will the king. King Alexander is furious that the traitor arranged for another to hang for his crimes. He wants him brought to justice. The man almost forced my cousin into a marriage he did not want, and once the betrothal was called off, convinced the Buchan to attack the Ramsays. This happened after being warned not to by the king.

"Now we have witnesses to MacNiven's attempted attack on the Grants. Uncle Logan traveled to the king just to update him and receive his instructions. There is the slim possibility that MacNiven would have been caught by another, but I doubt it. I'm quite sure he will arrive to tell us we're going after him. Truly we wait to see in which direction to travel."

"Then Ashlyn might have a wee bit of trouble on our trip unless we can find the fool who shot at her." Magnus hunched his shoulders up. "But somehow, I think she'll handle it."

"Aye," Jake chuckled. "But can you handle her? Sometimes my sire's wisdom amazes me."

"Wisdom? I wish he'd chosen another to watch her." He had to turn away a wee bit as he said it.

"You may fool yourself, but you're not fooling me, old friend," Jake whispered, clasping his friend's shoulder. "My sire chose exactly the right person for this job. I just wish I were going along to see it, but Aline and I need to stay here with her wee sisters."

"The lass will not make it easy on me, I fear, but I'll do my best to make you and your sire proud."

"You will." Jake spun on the heel of his boot and started heading back toward the lists. His next words were spoken over his shoulder. "I do not envy your trip, but I do look forward to the tales of your travels." There was a laugh in his voice. "Until then, I'll see what I can find out about our sour-bellied guard."

Magnus couldn't come up with a response before Jake was out of hearing distance. Aye, his friend was right. Ashlyn would keep him busy and make sure his guard was never relaxed.

She would be a challenge, but Magnus was starting to discover he loved challenges.

Ashlyn broke into a run once she was close to her family's hut on the loch. They were at the opposite end of the swimming area Alex had created after seeing his sister's beautiful swimming area at Clan Ramsay. Sibling competition, her stepsire had called it.

This was Ashlyn's favorite place in the world. Her mother and Robbie had fixed up the cottage for the four of them, but their family had expanded, and the original cottage had been too small to include Roddy and Padraig. Robbie's brothers and a few carpenters in the clan had helped him add two additions to the building: one new room for Ashlyn and Gracie and one for Roddy and Padraig. Roddy had moved over to the warriors' building, however, and Padraig would be going soon.

Ashlyn's mother, who had been trained by the renowned healer Lady Brenna Ramsay, still functioned as the clan's healer, which meant she was away from home more often than not.

As she stepped onto the porch they used to skin fish and enjoy the view of the loch, Ashlyn noticed how quiet it was. "Mama?" She stepped inside and found her mother tearing linen strips. Gracie, who often helped her in her healing work, stood at her side.

"Good day to you, Ashlyn. How was your archery practice?"

Gracie glanced up and smiled but said nothing. She had never been much of a talker. She spent most of her time with their mother, for the Grant lass closest to her in age, Kyla, was very different from her in temperament. Ashlyn thought that Eliza and Gracie would be much alike, but the laird's second-born daughter was much younger—her hips were just beginning to broaden, and Gracie was twenty summers. It was a marriageable age, but Gracie never mentioned marriage.

"It was not the best. May we talk?"

"Of course. Is something bothering you?" Caralyn finished with her duties, then sat at the large table in the center of the chamber. She pointed to the chair across from hers. "Come sit with me. I have not talked with you much since you decided to join the Grant guards in their search for MacNiven. Do you not have some misgivings about traveling with a large group of men?"

Ashlyn sighed and flopped into the chair with a huff. "I was not worried, but it seems I should be."

"Why?" She reached over and ran her fingers through Ashlyn's long locks. "Ashlyn, if you choose not to plait your hair, you must at least run a comb through it, or it will become too unruly." Ashlyn's mama's gaze carried down her dirty and disheveled clothing, but she said naught.

Gracie circled around the table to get a better look at her. "She appears to have been rolling in the dirt," she said with a wee smile.

"The truth is I have been rolling in the grass, but not by choice. Someone was firing arrows at me on the archery field."

"What?" Caralyn jumped out of her chair, but then sat down again. "Something tells me I should be sitting when I hear your story."

"Someone else was shooting their bow, and I was almost hit by several arrows. Magnus came along and knocked me onto the ground to keep me from getting hit." She rubbed at her elbow, only then noticing that it bled a bit.

Her mother reached for a cloth and dipped it into the water basin before washing the wound with it. "Aye, remind me to thank Magnus, will you please?"

"This has happened before, Mama. There are lads that do not want me at the archery field. I think the intention was to frighten me, not hurt me, but Magnus told me something else that concerns me."

"I wish you would tell our laird this. He needs to know if someone is firing at you."

"I'll not tell Uncle Alex or he may order me to stay home, and I'm asking you not to say aught to him or anyone. 'Tis a private matter." Ashlyn scrunched her face in frustration and said, "There are men who are upset that a lass will be traveling as a guard. Magnus told me to be careful."

Caralyn gasped, her hand covering her mouth. "We must tell Robbie."

"Nay, I do not want to involve him. They'll only get more upset with me. I just wish to have your opinion." She took the cloth from her mother and used it to wipe the other spots on her face that needed it.

"Well, no woman has ever traveled with the Grant guards," her mother said. "I suppose there would be some who would think you do not belong."

Gracie asked, "I worry about you going alone with a group of men, Ashlyn."

"I will not be alone. Jamie and Braden are going. They'll stand up for me, as will Magnus."

"You must be careful. Many men believe women exist only to attend to their needs."

"I am already aware of that sad truth, Mama, you need not convince me of it." She rolled her eyes as she handed the cloth back to her mother.

"And how would you know that, daughter?" her mother asked, catching her gaze. "Your stepsire does not believe that nonsense, and neither do your uncles. Did something happen when you were young that you need to tell me about? We've discussed this before, and you've always denied any ill treatment. Were you being truthful?"

Slud. She hadn't intended to speak so frankly. It had to be Magnus's fault for clouding her mind with odd thoughts. "Nay, Mama. Naught happened." She'd carry the memories to her grave. Her mother could never know.

"Ashlyn? I do not believe you. Tell me, please."

Ashlyn glanced over at her sister, her gaze catching all that took place in front of her. She hated bringing up the past to Gracie because she had been young enough to have no memories at all. It was best for Gracie if it stayed that way. She did not share her memories with anyone. "I have told you before that I watched the cruel Norseman beat you. 'Tis why I do not wish to marry." Ashlyn averted her gaze from her mother and sister, hoping her lie would not be apparent. Truth was that she'd thought about marriage and bairns frequently of late, but she would never admit it to anyone.

"Yet you continue to have nightmares." She could tell by the look in her mother's eyes that she didn't believe her, but Ashlyn could not—would not—give her what she wanted. Why dwell on the past? Robbie Grant had saved them from all that, and she would always love him for it. Gracie had been so young she could not remember a life before Clan Grant, and though Ashlyn envied her, she was grateful her little sister could live a normal life.

Her mother whispered, "I'll leave it be for now. But someday, I hope you'll confide in me. Otherwise, the past will continue to haunt you."

Ashlyn got up from her chair so she could escape that look in her mother's eyes.

Her memories already haunted her. She hoped going on this journey would help wash them away.

# CHAPTER THREE

Magnus moved through the forest, surveying the twigs around him to find ones that were the right size. As soon as he had a handful, he strode out of the forest and into the strath. He loved taking his dogs into the wide valley so they could run freely. The trees were bare, waiting for winter snows to come in as they did every year. He wondered if Ashlyn had considered the fact that this trip could keep them out of the Highlands for a while if heavy snow fell while they were in Edinburgh.

His dogs eagerly awaited him. Though he threw two of the sticks in opposite directions, both dogs chased down the first one. He shook his head, chuckling at the dogs' antics.

"Mada, Sim, can you not each chase your own stick?"

Sim made it to the stick first, and he hastily grabbed it in his teeth and ran back to Magnus. Mada seemed to droop in disappointment, but then he raised his head and searched the grounds for a second twig to bring to his master.

Sim dropped the twig at Magnus's feet, panting with his tongue lolling out to the side. Mada rushed up moments later and dropped the puny stick he'd found next to Sim's, who promptly bent down to take a sniff.

"Always competing against each other, are you not?" He picked up two larger twigs and heaved them in the same direction, sending both beasts off.

Magnus sat down on a nearby rock and watched his two beloved animals. Torrian Ramsay had brought them to him as pups after Rhona's death. His friend's intention had undoubtedly been for the dogs to help restore Magnus's broken heart. That had seemed impossible at the time, but Magnus had been so very lonely. He'd agreed to take one; Torrian had refused to split the brothers up. So Magnus had kept the two Deerhounds with a grumble. Now he could not be happier to have them in his life. The dogs rushed over with the larger sticks and sat in front of him, awaiting his next command. Magnus patted his leg and the two rushed up on either side of him for their favorite, a rub behind their ears.

While the dogs had not come close to replacing his dear wife, they had filled a gap in his life, giving him a reason to get up every day, and forcing him to smile. Not that smiling was difficult for Magnus, he smiled naturally almost all the time, but with the two dogs around, his smile was more reflective of his actual mood. He was also glad that Torrian had forced two on him instead of one, because at least they had each other when Magnus had to travel with the warriors. There were two lads nearby that cared for his dogs when he was gone, but he did not feel bad about leaving the dogs alone together.

Mada barked, tearing Magnus's attention away from his thoughts. Robbie Grant was approaching him. Robbie waved to Magnus as he made his way down the hill from his cottage, and the two dogs took off after him, recognizing the friendly face and anxious for more greetings and ear rubs.

Magnus leaned back on the rock, hoping the sun would emerge and warm his face. The cold nights of the Highland winters had started, though today was not bad. "Robbie, what brings you out to my area of Grant land?" His smile went from ear to ear, guessing this visit might have something to do with his Ashlyn.

*His* Ashlyn? Had he really thought that?

Robbie came over to his side and plunked down on a nearby rock. "The rocks are getting too cold these days, are they not, Magnus? Or is your arse so tough that you have no feeling?"

"Aye, the rock is cold. Keeps me alert. I have to stay ahead of my dogs. Do you need help with something? Must be important to come all the way over here."

"I'm here because my wife sent me. 'Tis not that far, just down the hill."

"Allow me to guess. I'd wager she's worried about Ashlyn traveling with the warriors."

"Aye, she is, as am I." Robbie scratched his head. "But we trust you, Magnus, and I told Caralyn that our laird made the right choice for Ashlyn. You will protect her."

"What concerns the two of you if not her safety?"

"Caralyn's worried about how Ashlyn will treat you."

Magnus leaned back on his elbows to stare up at the sky. "I appreciate your concern, but I think I can handle a wee lass like Ashlyn."

"I would not call Ashlyn wee, and I can tell you she's got some muscle behind her punch."

Magnus sat up. "Her punch?"

Robbie cleared his throat. "I do not wish to talk much about my wife's past, but I can tell you this much. Caralyn, Ashlyn, and Gracie were all around some unsavory characters before Caralyn met me. Gracie remembers naught, but some of Ashlyn's memories still bother her."

"I know, we all know, she does not like to be touched, and I respect that. Is there more I should know?" Magnus threw the sticks again to keep the dogs busy, then pushed back on the rock.

"She often wakes up in the middle of a nightmare swinging."

"Swinging?"

"Punching. As her protector, you will likely sleep close to her, so I must warn you that when she awakens from one of her night terrors, she'll swing her fists at anyone who comes near her. And I can tell you from experience that she has some strength behind those punches in the middle of the night."

"And she's never said what ails her?"

"Nay. We've tried many times, but she always blames it on the Norseman who attacked her mother. Caralyn thinks there is more to it, and so do I." He wiped a hand over his face. "'Tis horrible to see. She swings her arm over her head as though she were stabbing someone."

"Hellfire, how can the lass sleep restfully if her sleep is that disturbed? Does it happen often?" Magnus couldn't imagine what it would be like to have recurring dreams about an enemy for years. He'd vowed to find out the truth of what had happened to Ashlyn, but did he have any chance if she wouldn't tell her mother or her sister?

"Do not worry, my lord," Magnus said. "I vow to help Ashlyn, and am not worried about how hard she hits me. If I can take Jake and Jamie's pummeling…"

"And Loki's?"

"Aye," Magnus laughed. "And Loki's. They've all pummeled me before."

"True, because you are older, and you grew before they did, and your arms are the size of tree trunks. They would not have lasted long in one-on-one combat if you'd fought back."

Magnus guffawed. "It did amuse me when the three of them would try to take me down together. But then they grew up, and I had to admit I could no longer handle the three of them at once."

"That was one of Jamie's favorite days," Robbie said with a grin. "He loved that they'd finally beaten you."

"Aye, but Jake still tried to beat me on his own. He can best me with a sword or a bow, but not hand-to-hand combat."

Robbie stood up. "My thanks for reminding me of that. The lads tried to get you to spar with them every day, did they not?"

"Sometimes. But sometimes the bruises would worry my Rhona, so I would back away for a while."

"You still miss her terribly, aye?"

Magnus sighed. "Aye. The dogs are company, but 'tis not the same."

"Mayhap you should think of taking another wife. Rhona was taken from you way too young. I cannot imagine how difficult it was to lose both your wife and son."

Magnus leaned his elbows on his knees and stared at the ground. "I wish I dared to love another, but the truth is I'm afraid. The loss was too painful for me to bear it again."

"I hope you will feel differently with time. Caralyn completes me." Robbie brushed the dirt off his clothing.

They both stared at the dogs as they chased each other across the meadow. "My lord…" Magnus began.

"Magnus, I am not your lord, so there's no need for such formality."

"Aye, but you deserve the respect due the laird's brother. My lord, I promise to handle Ashlyn carefully. She cannot hurt me with her fists."

"Her mother and I both hope she will not hurt you with her words either. She can be quite harsh at times."

"I appreciate the warning, but I'll wager Ashlyn and I will get along quite well."

Magnus had a feeling this trip would prove to be quite interesting.

Ashlyn closed the door in the messenger's face and turned toward her mother. "We're wanted in the solar. Uncle Logan is here."

"I know you are excited, Ashlyn, but you could have treated the messenger a wee bit better. He traveled all the way out here in the cold wind." Caralyn gave her a stern look.

She swung the door wide open, but the lad had already jumped on his horse and departed. "Forgive me, Mama. I was not thinking."

"You will remember your manners, whether you are traveling with the guards or not. I raised you right. Do not lose sight of that."

"Aye, Mama. Do you wish to go to the keep with me?"

Caralyn stared at her daughter, her arms crossed. "I know not what I should do, daughter. We are verra different, though I do not love you any less for it. Mayhap I should let you go alone. 'Twill only worry me to hear what your uncle is planning."

Ashlyn frowned at first, but it was true that she and her mama had dissimilar interests. And her mama had said she loved her. "Mama, I must know I have your support, but you need not go to the keep with me if you'd rather stay here."

"If I understood the dangers you shall face, I would not be able to sleep at night. Yet I know 'tis best for me to allow you to do what you must." Tears misted her lashes. "Ashlyn, I just wish you would confide in me. I know there is more than you tell me."

"Mama, I'm fine. Do not worry. Please." She hugged her mother before she grabbed her small satchel and mantle. "I shall return."

"I will await you here. I'm sure your da will be there." She hugged Ashlyn, then spun around and reclaimed her chair near the hearth.

Ashlyn headed out the door toward the small stable where they kept their few horses. She hoped Uncle Logan had come with answers. Her sleep had been troubled by worry about those lasses who had disappeared from Castle Dubh. True, Aline had said they were not the nicest people, but everyone deserved to be safe.

What had happened to Lorna and Cedrica? What was MacNiven doing with them?

She rode to the keep, her head full of thoughts of what was to come. Would she be accepted as a true warrior?

Once inside the great hall, she drew a deep breath and found her way to the solar. She knocked, and when she heard her laird's voice, she opened the door.

Uncle Logan addressed her first. "Good morn to you, Ashlyn. Come in, sit and chat with us. You may have insight into this conversation."

She moved to a stool at the edge of the room, glancing at the others who were present. Some she had expected to see; some were a surprise.

Uncle Alex said, "Lass, are you still interested in traveling with our guards?"

She nodded quickly. "Aye. Is there news?"

"Aye," Uncle Logan said. "King Alexander wants MacNiven found. I have assured him that the Grant warriors have already searched the area with no success, so he has asked that we assign a special team to flush him out of hiding, even if we must travel back to Edinburgh and the Buchans. He said he'll hang the man himself, especially if the blackguard has harmed any women and children."

Jake stood up and said, "We've chosen a team of eight to follow Uncle Logan. Jamie will be the lead, the others are Magnus, Ashlyn, Braden, Art, Coll, Osgar, and Tormod. We shall send more if more are needed."

"Good choices, Chief," Uncle Logan smiled. "Ashlyn, Jamie, and Magnus will be invaluable for their previous dealings with the bastard. We leave by dawn because we wish to get as far south as possible before the deep snows prevent it. Be ready to go. Any questions?"

Uncle Logan scanned the group. "I'd also like to add to prepare your families for the possibility that if we spend much time in the south, we may run into enough snow on our way back to prevent us from coming through until spring."

"The lass goes with us?" Coll asked with a furrowed forehead.

"Aye," Art added. "Will she not be a hindrance?"

Osgar snorted. "For sure."

Alex Grant stood and stared down at them from his great height. "You speak of my niece who works as hard at archery as any of you. The next man who questions my judgment shall be relieved of his assignment and replaced. Now, I'll ask again. Any questions?"

Ashlyn somehow managed to contain both her outrage and her smirk.

"Nay," Coll said, his face reddening.

"Nay, my laird. My thanks for the assignment," Tormod said.

"I accept your decision, my laird," Art added. "No disrespect was intended."

"Nay," Osgar said. "No more questions."

"Fine. Ready yourselves to meet at the stables at first light." Uncle Logan nodded toward the men, dismissing them. The guardsmen all left, but each of them cast a glance at Ashlyn on their way out. Only family remained in the room—Ashlyn, her stepsire, Magnus, Jamie, Jake, Uncle Alex, and Uncle Logan.

"You left Gwyneth behind?" Uncle Alex asked.

"Aye, we'll meet up with her at the royal castle. She has gone to Ramsay land to retrieve Sorcha and Molly. My plan is to search every sign of activity on the way south, and to travel to Edinburgh if we need to do so. I do not expect to see MacNiven in Edinburgh because he would be easily recognized, but we must be open to any possibility. 'Tis quite possible that he has gone to Buchan for protection."

"Magnus is assigned as Ashlyn's protector?" Robbie asked, glancing at her.

Jamie and Jake both answered simultaneously. "Aye."

"Is there any other way?" Ashlyn asked.

Every man in the room spoke this time. "Nay."

Every man except Magnus. He just smiled.

# CHAPTER FOUR

Magnus stayed behind after Ashlyn hurried out. He had a good idea where she was headed, so he'd catch up with her in a few minutes. "I think we shall find some hard feelings from the other guards, and I do not know how Ashlyn will handle it. I'll make sure they do not touch her."

"I agree," Jake said, nodding. "I think there's something brewing among the guards, though I do not know what. I want someone I trust there to handle the situation."

Robbie clasped Magnus's shoulder. "You'll have your hands full with her, but I believe 'twill be an interesting journey."

"If I did not believe she could be an asset to the search, I would not send her," Alex said. "But she has an instinct that we, as men, do not possess. We must take advantage of it. And with women involved, we may need a woman along. I think it is a sound plan." Alex stood from his chair. "I wish you luck. Send a messenger with aught you uncover."

Magnus said, "Aye, my laird. We shall be successful. Jake, I know you have a new wife, so go enjoy your family. We shall see you soon."

He said his goodbyes and left, hurrying as soon as he hit the outdoor air. He would wager Ashlyn had headed to the archery field to practice her skills one more time before they left, and he feared one of the guardsmen had followed her.

He found a horse and headed out to the practice field, only to hear a scream from a distance. His heart in his throat, he flicked the reins and galloped out. As soon as he arrived, he jumped off his horse. It only took him a few moments to find Ashlyn, who was hiding behind a large rock at the periphery of the field.

"What is it?" he asked, panting from the exertion. He knew something had happened because of her color. She was pale as a linen square, and being a woman who loved the outdoors, her cheeks were usually flushed and rosy.

"Someone fired at me again. I was practicing and an arrow flew by me."

"How close?"

"It missed me, but it still upsets me. I searched the area for the archer, but they must have left when they saw you. I have not seen another arrow."

"They? There was more than one?"

"Nay. I think only one. Why are you here?"

"Because I was sure you would come out here, and I felt the tension in the room from Osgar, Tormod, Coll, and Art."

"You think one of them is responsible? But they have no reason to want to hurt me. They were all chosen for the voyage."

"Lass, I do not think their aim is to hurt you or kill you. I think they seek to frighten you into staying home. The only reason your cousin agreed not to tell his sire is because we believe you will leave the guilty party behind. If you refuse the assignment, then several others could possibly take your place."

"Whatever the situation, they are gone now. I'm going back to practice." She jumped up from her spot, peered around at the trees, and strode back over to her usual spot.

"Foolish lass!" Magnus yelled, making it to his feet in time to follow her. As soon as they made their way to the middle of the field, he heard the very sound he had dreaded, the swish of an arrow flying through the air. His movements were trained from many years as a warrior. He dove for Ashlyn, his arms wrapping around her to knock her out of the way.

Ashlyn's reaction was instinctual. As soon as they hit the ground together, she shoved at him, though she couldn't move him because he was on top of her. "Get away! How dare you touch me! Leave me be." She pummeled and shoved him as best she could until he finally rolled off her.

"Leave you be? If I had not pulled you down, the arrow could have pierced your skull."

"That arrow was not even close, and you do not have permission to touch me. You can yell at me or shove me, but do not ever land on top of me again." She jumped to her feet.

He joined her. "I'll land on you whenever I deem it necessary. I cannot allow you to be foolish. Whether your attacker means to kill you or nay, you could still lose your life. This is my assignment as a Grant guard, and I do not take it lightly."

Ashlyn was more furious at him than the situation warranted, and he found himself thinking about what Robbie had said to him. Something had scarred this lass and left her with a fear of being touched. She hadn't stepped far away, but as soon as she heard his comment, she came at him again.

"You will not!" she bellowed. "Do you hear me? You cannot touch me whenever you deem it necessary." She swung and caught him in the arm.

Magnus kept his hands at his sides, refusing to swing back. He did not hit women.

"I will have to touch you, and you better learn how to deal with it while we're away."

"Nay, you will not. Do not touch me. Never touch me. Never, ever. Who do you think you are? Do you think you're a Norseman?" Her hands connected with his chest again, slapping at him.

Magnus could tell when the tears began to fuel her actions. Suddenly, she was no longer Ashlyn the strong archer; she was a wee lassie fighting someone bigger and stronger. A Norseman maybe, or some other demon from her past.

Her voice even rose to a higher pitch. "Leave me be. You cannot touch me. Do not touch me. Go back to your own country." Tears trickled down her cheeks as she swung at him. She connected, but her light swings weren't hurting him.

Magnus held his arms out and whispered, "Go ahead, lass. Get it out of you. Let that bad man have all your fury."

"Just because you are a man, you think you can touch me as you wish. You cannot. I will not let you. My da would not allow it if he were still here, but he left us." Her slaps turned to fists as she continued to lightly pummel Magnus's chest, tears running down her cheeks.

Magnus said naught, allowing her to have her way. This was a wee lass swinging at him, not Ashlyn, the fighter. Someone had violated her, and he was determined to find out who—but first he would allow her the opportunity to rid herself of her anger.

Her demeanor suddenly changed. It was as if she were awakening to the present moment. "Why? Why are you letting me hit you? Stop me. I should not be hitting you."

But she swung again, a weak attempt to hit him, and finally she gave in to the tears. Falling to the ground in a heap, she cradled her face in her hands and sobbed, her whole body shaking with emotion.

Magnus scanned the area again to make sure any threat to her safety was gone, but he was confident her attacker had left. Where did he go from here?

He let her cry, hoping it would help her to heal. Eventually, he sat down next to her and reached over to tuck a lock of hair behind her ear.

She leaned away from him but drew her gaze up to his. "What are you doing?"

"I'm trying to help you. 'Tis all. May I comfort you? Do you wish to cry on my shoulder?"

"Nay, and I do not need comforting." Her scowl told him she meant what she said.

How different she was from his Rhona, who had loved being comforted by him.

He reached for the stray hair again and whispered, "Ashlyn, this will not hurt you. You have a leaf in your hair."

She allowed him that small touch, and he could see the tension leave her body.

"Who was it, Ashlyn? Who hurt you?"

She closed her eyes, reigning in her sobs to a hiccup. "No one."

"I do not believe you. Was it a Norseman?"

"Magnus, when I was eight summers, I watched a man almost beat my mother to death. I hid behind a rock and made my sister turn the other way, but I could not." She stared off into the trees, mopping at her wet cheeks with a linen square she had pulled from her satchel.

Magnus whispered, "I would not have been able to look away either. Do not be upset with yourself for watching; you were too small to help her. Did he touch you?"

She shook her head. "He punched her in the belly, then in the face, then dragged her across the stone beach so fast it tore her skin off. I watched her try to fight back, but she couldn't. It was as if she could not feel anything he did. Do you know what he wished to do with her?"

"Nay, but I think I can guess. You need not explain."

She brought her gaze to his, and her brown eyes held a fury he'd not seen often. "You think he wished to force himself on her, but you probably did not guess that he planned to give her to all his friends on the boat after he finished with her."

Magnus reached for her hand, but she pulled it back. "Lass…how can you know that?"

"Because I knew all about sex back then. I knew what it meant to see a man rub his crotch. That's what several of them did on the galley ship. Though I could not understand their words they shouted at her, I knew what they intended to do to her."

"But they did not, Ashlyn. Your mother fought them off."

Her tears started again. "I saw him punch her and her head hit a rock and she did not move. I thought she was dead. I ran back to Gracie because she had started to cry, and when I returned to peek around the rock, there were more men. Men everywhere. They chased the Norseman back to his ship. One of them was Robbie, but I did not know at the time that he was there to save my mother. I thought he was another attacker. I saw his big sword and got scared and ran with Gracie. We hid closer to the beach. I was so frightened, and we had little to eat."

"But your mother survived, and so did you and Gracie."

"Aye, she did. She is a strong woman. Now you know what troubles me, so you need not ask again."

"Aye, I can see why that would trouble anyone."

She stood up from her spot and moved over to nuzzle her horse.

Magnus helped her mount, and when she turned her horse around, he stopped her.

"Ashlyn, when you're ready to tell me about the man who touched you, I'll be ready to listen."

She frowned, narrowing her gaze at him before she flicked the reins of her horse, shooting off toward the loch.

She was not fooling him one bit.

Ashlyn decided to stop and visit with Effie, Aline's friend and another former prisoner at Castle Dubh, to see if she had recalled any more information about MacNiven. Magnus had unnerved her in more ways than one. First of all, how had he guessed there was more to her story? Of course, she'd never tell him the rest. She'd never told anyone.

But what bothered her most was her reaction to him. Her instinct had been to allow him to hold her until her tears ended. In fact, she had thrown herself to the ground to fight the impulse. And he had touched her…more than once. He had touched her, and she had survived. In fact, she had almost wanted him to touch her cheek. Aye, when he'd removed the leaf from her hair, she had fought the urge to lean in to him.

What was happening to her?

*Forget it.* There were more important matters to attend to. First, she decided to find out as much information as she could about the MacNiven and his despicable, though thankfully dead, ally Hew Gordon. Then she needed to pack her satchel.

She'd already packed her satchel five times, but another time wouldn't hurt, at least to make sure she hadn't forgotten anything. Aye, Magnus was unimportant today.

There was already a second horse tied up outside Effie's cottage. Moments after she knocked on the door, it was flung open by Maisie and Morna, both giggling. Aline's wee sisters had recovered remarkably well from their ordeal at Castle Dubh. How she loved watching the lassies play, just as she'd loved watching her younger brothers play. Aye, she did want her own family, but how could she? Would she ever be able to let go of her fears? Would her nightmares ever stop? Was there a man she could trust?

"Ashlyn, come visit with us," Maisie said as the two lassies grabbed her hands and tugged her inside.

After closing the door behind her, Ashlyn picked up the lassies one at a time and swung them in a circle before she set them down, but as soon as she set Maisie down, Effie's daughter Una scuttled up, eager for her turn. When she finished greeting the girls, Aline said, "Lassies, play with your animals for a moment. We must talk with Ashlyn."

When the bairns retrieved their toys and scampered over to the hearth, Ashlyn sat down at the table with Aline and Effie.

"Jake told me you are leaving on the morrow," Aline whispered. "I cannot believe 'tis happening so soon. Are you not nervous about being the only lass among so many warriors?"

"Nay, I can handle myself. I'm good with a bow, though not as good as Aunt Gwyneth or Molly and Sorcha. But I was hoping you two could tell me everything you remember about Ranulf MacNiven." She looked from Aline to Effie. "Where did Hew Gordon get his wealth?"

Aline sighed, then said, "I'll tell you all I know, and Effie can add aught she recalls. Hew inherited his wealth from his sire. He had two sacks of coins hidden under the floorboards in his chamber. MacNiven stole the largest of the bags, heavy with coin, and Hew was beside himself even though he had another small bag hidden."

"Where did his sire get the coins?"

"I'm not really sure, and I do not think Effie knows either." She glanced at Effie, who shook her head. "But in the past year, I overheard Hew talking with his guards about how much money he could make if he had concubines for all the men in the Highlands. One of the guards reminded him of how slow business would be in the winter, so Hew planned to move closer to the Lowlands to avoid the bite of the cold. Someone he knew once hired several women to service men and told him how easy it was to get coin for good-looking women if they were trained in the seductive arts. I do not think this was discussed with MacNiven. He wished to keep all his wealth to himself, just hire MacNiven for protection."

"I often heard him say he was training us," Effie whispered. "My skin crawls to think of laying with a different man every night."

"Then why the wee lassies?" Ashlyn glanced over her shoulder to make sure the bairns were not listening to them.

Aline lowered her voice, her gaze fixed on her sister, Maisie. "He kept them to help control us. One of his men advised him that some men would buy young lasses, but Hew said he wouldn't do that to a bairn—they had to be over ten and four. He said he'd keep them until then, always have new ones growing. He had visions of an entire castle dedicated to men's pleasures. Wine, whisky, whores, whatever they wanted."

"Ashlyn," Effie said, "I...I haven't felt strong enough to ask before now, but why are you going after this MacNiven? He and Hew argued all the time. They were not friends. Hew was the one guilty of stealing women, not MacNiven. He was only interested in battle and land. He wanted the power of the Highlands and all the Grant guards."

"Ranulf MacNiven was a chieftain of his own castle, but he attacked my cousins, the Ramsays, when King Alexander had told him not to do so. During the attack, one of Buchan's sons was killed, so the king declared the attack an act of treason. He sentenced MacNiven to death by hanging, but it would seem he switched places with another. He ran to the Highlands in the hopes he'd never be caught. That's why everyone at Castle Dubh knew him by a different name."

"Until Jake recognized him." Aline stared at her needlework, a faraway look in her gaze.

"Aye, that helps me understands why the Grant warriors must pursue him, but why must *you* go, Ashlyn? Why risk everything to chase him?" Effie drummed her fingers on the table.

"Because I did not like the things I heard when I was spying in Castle Dubh. I heard discussions that Hew had sent some girls to a friend because he was afraid the Grants would attack and he would not be able to save all the lasses. He had promised one that she would be in charge of the others. And since Hew is now dead, where are Lorna and Cedrica? I think MacNiven knows where they are. Though he did not like Gordon, I believe he paid close attention to everything he did. While I didn't like them, they have a right to choose their life, not be forced against their will."

Aline said, "It sounds as if each man wished to use Lorna and Cedrica for his own purposes. But MacNiven must have won. He must know where they are."

Ashlyn grabbed Effie's hand. "Don't you see, Effie? I need to do this. MacNiven and his men are bad men, and we have no idea what he is up to now. He may not have been directly involved with Hew Gordon and the women, but he may have taken over some of Hew's plans. Aunt Gwyneth was almost sold by men like MacNiven many years ago. Mayhap he is doing the same with Lorna and Cedrica. We do not know for sure, but he is running from the king, so my guess is he will do aught to survive. We must stop him, and we must do it now."

Aline and Effie hung their heads as they all stared at the three wee lassies playing in the corner. A moment later, Aline whispered, "Thank the Lord above for Jake Grant. I could not imagine a worse fate."

"I know you were not fond of Lorna and Cedrica," Ashlyn whispered, "but I will not rest until I find them. Once I find MacNiven, I'll put an arrow in his black heart for all the trouble he's caused my clan."

# CHAPTER FIVE

Magnus rubbed the sleep from his eyes as he made his way to the stables. Usually a sound sleeper, he'd had many thoughts in the middle of the night of a lass with rich brown eyes. She'd actually shared some of her past with him, which pleased him greatly. It was the first step in getting her to trust him. He would continue his attempt to break through her barriers. Ashlyn stood next to her horse, arranging her belongings on the saddle for their journey. He decided it best to speak with her right away.

"Good morn to you, Ashlyn." He stopped to rub the neck of her horse.

"Good morn. I do not need your help, I am fine." Her gaze caught his for a moment before it returned to her horse.

It didn't take long to recognize that her barriers were back in place. "I am well aware that you can take care of yourself. You need not remind me, but mayhap 'tis best for you to get it out of your system before we leave."

"Get what out of my system?" She turned to give him her full attention, her hands on her full hips, hips he'd loved to grab onto.

"Your dislike of lads, or mayhap 'tis just me. Either way, I must stay close to you on this journey, so get all your distaste out now. It will make our journey easier."

He noticed the fury in her eyes, and he did his best to hide his smile, though that was difficult to do since he was so accustomed to putting on a smile. And he certainly did not release the laughter that formed in his gut when he saw the look of indignation in her eyes.

When he was young, he'd overheard his father tell his mother how much he loved her smile, so he'd practiced his own smile ever since until it had become part of his nature. His mother had told him smiling would make his day better, and he kept that thought close to his heart.

"I do not dislike lads. I just do not want them to touch me. Why is that so hard for you and the others to understand? Just keep your hands to yourself, and we'll get along fine."

"Because someday you'll understand that we are not all out to hurt you, lass. I understand that some lads, or mayhap many lads, caused you pain in your past, but 'twas not me. I would never hurt you. Hopefully, someday you'll realize that." Magnus spun on his heel and headed into the stable to saddle his horse.

The stable lads were busy, so he readied his own horse for travel. The place was a bustle of activity because many of the clanspeople had come to wish them well, and the youngest lads loved to chase the warriors through the meadow as a send-off. Jake, who was part of the crowd, wove his way toward Magnus.

"Getting your ears chewed off this early in the morn, my friend?" Jake's smirk told Magnus that the other man had seen him sparring with Ashlyn.

"Och, the lass must learn to trust me."

"If anyone can convince her to do that, 'tis you. Just be wary. Ashlyn has been trained by Gwyneth, who's still one of the best…"

"Not one of the best, but *the* best, even after all these years. And she's also one hell of a trainer. You saw how her son fought at Castle Dubh."

"Aye, but allow me to make my point. Ashlyn was trained to shoot, but she has not been trained in strategizing. It also worries me that she has made this mission too personal. How this fits in with her past, I do not know, but be wary."

"You could be right about that. She is quite determined to take him down."

"If I am right, I fear that she may not be able to keep her bow straight when she is faced with MacNiven. I think of Uncle Logan's stories of when Aunt Gwyneth fought the man who killed her father and brother…"

Magnus sighed. "Aye, Gwyneth was so upset, she missed her target several times. I have heard her talk about it."

"And I am suggesting that Ashlyn may react the same way. I

love my cousin. Watch over her. When she is close to MacNiven, she may lose her ability to kill him with her arrow."

He nodded. "I will be mindful of that happening." His horse was ready, so he led him out of the stables. Jake followed him toward the group that had gathered in front of the stables. He squeezed Magnus's shoulder. "Godspeed, and if anyone can help Ashlyn, 'tis you, my friend."

Magnus guffawed. "You can count on it, my lord."

Ashlyn forced herself to smile at Magnus, who was riding beside her. After he'd left her earlier to go to the stables, she'd thought about all he'd said. Aye, Magnus was not the one who'd forced her to travel with a protector. The man had a good heart, and she needed to be mindful of it.

She did not want a protector, but at least Magnus would be respectful.

Her stepsire's parting words had settled in her mind after their departure. "Ashlyn, be kind to those men. They are the ones who will fight alongside you. You must trust them, or you will be in danger if you ride into battle." Robbie was correct. Her mother had said something similar to her the eve before: "You must trust Magnus. Who else can you trust? Jamie leads the group, and your cousin Braden is young. You must have someone there who will assist you at all times."

She had wished to argue that she could take care of herself, but the farther they traveled from Grant land, the heavier the truth settled on her. It was just the eight of them. Well, ten more guards were traveling the periphery, acting as both lookouts and protection, but there were seven lads she would have to fight alongside if the situation arose.

She was a Grant guard now—the first lass in her clan to earn that honor. Her mission was to fight for her king, her clan, her laird, and her fellow warriors. The thought humbled her. She vowed to stop arguing with Magnus. Her mother was right. She needed someone to trust and depend on, especially if there were those who did not wish her to travel with the guards, and Magnus was the best choice.

Magnus quirked a brow at her. "Feeling more kindly, lass?"

"Aye." How exactly should she explain her state of mind? "I've vowed to make the best of it. I also trust you will assist me once we've uncovered MacNiven's whereabouts."

"You have the right of it. I will always be here to help you, no matter what the circumstances."

With those few words, a calm silence settled between them until they stopped midday to take care of their needs and grab some fare. Ashlyn's mind was made up. She vowed not to slow the group because of the amount of time it would take her to attend to her needs. Her mother had given her that bit of wisdom before she'd left, and Ashlyn had understood it to be true.

After all, she'd caught her brothers, Roddy and Padraig, practicing their aim in the snow behind the cottage when they were four and six summers.

It was then she'd realized the true injustice of her station as a lass. They could relieve themselves in less than a minute. Well, she'd already stashed some of her favorite leaves in her satchel, and she'd go as fast as she could. Under no circumstance would she be the last to emerge from the trees whenever they stopped. She would not give her comrades the chance to complain about her.

She rushed into the bushes, not going far because her skirts would conceal her modesty. She finished her business, heard a few crude remarks that she ignored, then ran back to her horse, only to find out that she was still the last one there. Staring at the ground, she patted her horse, hoping naught was said to her.

And it wasn't. Naught was said to her about her time in the bushes, but the lads had started a different conversation. She must have arrived in the middle of it, because Coll was speaking animatedly to Jamie with his hand on his hip.

"She needs to plait it, Jamie, and you know it. If you wish to bring a female along, it suits me as long as she is not easily identifiable as a female. You know the reivers will go for a woman."

Coll shot a look at them before turning to fuss with his belongings behind the saddle.

She turned her head back to Jamie to gauge his response. Plaiting her hair was a chore she hated. Her unruly brown hair fell to her waist in wild waves that were so difficult to contain. Aye, her mother was correct that she ought to comb it more often, but it took so long. She'd begged her mother to cut it all off, but she'd refused, saying she did not wish to make Ashlyn any more laddish.

That was a term she hated. She was not like a lad at all. Her breasts were large, and her hips were wide enough, though there was little flab in between because she'd always worked so hard outside. How could anyone mistake her for a lad? Still, her mother had wounded her vanity enough that she'd never cut her mane.

Jamie barked at Coll. "Your hair is flying in the wind too, Coll, so if you don't plait yours, neither should Ashlyn. She can make up her own mind."

"Jamie, you know how many reivers look for a female," Osgar added. "She'll cause us trouble. I agree with Coll. Either plait her hair or send her home."

"I have to agree with them, Jamie," Art said.

Magnus said, "She's fine without her hair plaited. Stop trying to cause trouble, Coll, and let's get on our way before the heavy snow flies."

Magnus had defended her, and a piece of her heart melted. At least, that's what the feeling in her chest felt like. He'd supported her and he was not her cousin or uncle. Did he know what that meant to her?

Jamie stared at the seven of them, waiting for them to listen. Her cousin had an uncanny ability to get people's attention.

"Ashlyn does not need to plait her hair. If anyone has trouble with that, then go back now while I still have the opportunity to pull from the periphery guards before we are too far south. You have one minute to make your decision. Mount up, and if you follow us, there'll be no more arguing about anyone's hair."

She heard some grumbling, but no one made any motion to head back. Magnus stepped up beside her to help her mount.

The journey was uneventful until later the next day. They'd reached the ravine that Ashlyn had always loved in the summer. The path was on the left, next to a tall wall of stone, and to the right was a small stream meandering over the rocks and through the trees. It was a beautiful sight, but she had always noticed the way the lead man in any group always tensed up before heading through the ravine. Many years had passed before she understood why.

It was the perfect place for an ambush. The path was narrow

and there was no way to take off into a meadow. There were only two directions to go: forward or backward. Reivers knew it, every clan knew it, and every lad knew it, which was why silence descended on the group as soon as they entered the ravine. Jamie led, but held his arm up to indicate the others should slow their horses and fall back a bit. He moved forward at a slow pace, making as little noise as possible.

Fear crept up the back of Ashlyn's neck, almost as if someone were running fingers lightly across her skin, moving upward. They could not ride abreast through the area. Jamie was first, Magnus behind him, then Ashlyn, Braden, Coll, Tormod, Art, and Osgar. Magnus hung back, waiting to get the all-clear sign from Jamie. They neared a spot that was hidden from the path completely—the perfect place for an attacker to lie in wait. She straightened, tipping her head to hear any sound at all, but the day was quiet except for the call of a rare bird.

Just like her Uncle Logan's. "Trap!" she shouted.

That was when chaos erupted. Two horses shot out from behind the rocks, aiming straight at them. Jamie and Magnus unsheathed their swords and headed straight for the attackers, Jamie taking the lead and Magnus going for the second. Ashlyn moved aside and positioned her bow for any shot she could get. Jamie cut his attacker down, as did Magnus, but four more lads replaced the first two, and shouting and yelling and war whoops rent the air as the horses were pulled in different directions. She shot one of the lads riding toward Jamie, taking the lout out with an arrow in his belly, and the would-be attacker's horse skidded to a stop, throwing him off.

Another warrior filled her view, so she nocked a second arrow. The lad shouted the one thing she'd hoped not to hear, "Get the lass!" He pointed directly at her.

She let her second arrow fly and heard it connect along with a scream of pain, but she never saw where it landed. A horse came from behind her, bringing its rider close enough to grab her around the waist and lift her onto his horse. All sorts of yelling met her ears, but she landed with enough of an oomph to distract her and take her breath away.

Too panicked to see or properly use her senses, she heard the lads around her—some friends, some foes—shouting.

"I've got her!"

"Take her out of here."

"Magnus, they've got Ash!"

"Bring her to the chief."

"Jamie, they're coming from behind, too. 'Twas an ambush."

"Ash, fight! Don't make it easy for him."

This last statement came from Magnus, and she could not agree more, but she had to calm her panic and get her wits working again. As soon as she regained some control, she took stock of her situation, assessing her kidnapper and the area around her.

His horse wore no colors, and they were galloping across the front of the ravine that opened to the meadow. Soon they were flying across the meadow. She'd been tossed face down across the horse in front of her attacker, so she fought to get upright, hoping to give herself a chance to fall off the horse or at least slow him down.

The only problem was she feared she would heave. She wished to vomit her guts all over the light snowfall that covered the ground. The more the horse's spine dug into her belly, the more she wished to vomit. She fought hard against the tears that threatened to escape. Living her worst nightmare, she couldn't think what to do. All she could think about was that she'd been kidnapped to take care of a man's needs. She would heave for sure.

The footfalls of at least two other horses echoed behind her, and then she heard the sound she needed to hear more than any other: "Ash, get up and fight!"

Magnus. She moved her right hand to try to get to her knife, but she couldn't reach it. Her hair flew all around her face blocking her vision. *Mo chreach*, as her cousin Jake would say, her hair was haunting her. Mayhap the lads had been right, loath though she was to admit it. Grabbing hold of her captor's leg, she gripped him as hard as she could and bit his leg through his trews, hard enough for him to bellow and strike her, but not before the element of surprise gave her a moment to push against him to sit up.

His fist caught her face just as she managed to sit up in front of the fool. Then the strangest sound she'd ever heard rang through the trees.

Magnus.

# CHAPTER SIX

*Hellfire, Ashlyn, fight!*

Those were the only words that came to mind as he gained ground on her attacker. If he could get her to sit up, he could jump and pull her off the horse. True, they'd both take a rough tumble onto the ground, but she'd be free.

Suddenly, the bastard bellowed as if in pain, and Ashlyn pushed against him to get herself into a sitting position. Then the lout did something Magnus couldn't tolerate. He punched her with his fist, square to her jaw. A bellow ripped from Magnus's insides—deeper and more furious than any sound he'd ever issued—he launched himself at her attacker, both arms spread wide enough to knock both his Ashlyn and the fool who'd taken her off the horse.

They flew in two different directions, and the horse ran off into the distance. Luckily, Magnus kept enough of a grip on Ashlyn's attacker that he followed him to the ground and landed on top of him with a whoosh. Magnus weighed enough to knock the wind out of the lad, which gave him enough time to put his fist in the bastard's face and pummel his belly before he stood up to unsheathe his sword.

The lout staggered up and went for his own sword, and they parried for but a moment before Magnus stuck his sword into his heart. Ashlyn's attacker fell to the ground, and gasping for air, Magnus pulled his sword out and wiped it in the snow before returning it to its sheath. The bastard had hit Ashlyn, causing him to lose all sense. He'd reacted with pure emotion, which was the worst way to react in a disaster.

But it didn't matter. The lad had hit Ashlyn with *his fist*.

Still panting from exertion, he turned around to find Ashlyn, only to see a blur coming directly at him. At the last minute, he held his arms up as the lass launched herself into them, tears running down her face. He couldn't have been more shocked.

He wrapped her into his warm embrace, quite pleased with how she felt in his arms. It was as if she belonged there.

She stood back and mumbled, "My thanks for coming after me. I do not know what I would have done if, if…"

He placed a finger against her lips. "Hush. It did not happen, and the only reason I was able to put an end to this was because you fought him. Did you hit him in his man parts or what?" He grinned from ear to ear as he brushed the tears off her cheeks.

"Nay, I bit him. 'Twas the only way I could sit up. And I need to plait my hair. 'Twas everywhere. I should cut it all off, 'tis so unruly."

"Your cousin is almost here." He turned his head to the side, indicating Jamie was almost upon them. "I'll plait it later for you. I did it every night for Rhona."

She stepped away from him before Jamie arrived. In the distance, Magnus could see Braden corralling the horses chewing on a hidden area of grass clear of snow.

"What the hell did you make of them, Magnus? The rest are gone, though seven," he glanced over Magnus's shoulder, "make that eight, are now dead. They had no colors, but they clearly wished for Ashlyn."

Ashlyn hung her head, obviously still shaken by the adventure. Though she'd seen much as a bairn, she had still led a sheltered life within their clan. Had their laird made a mistake in sending her along? Nay. Magnus believed she'd show her true value before they were done.

Jamie tipped his head to his cousin. "Nice job taking out the one who had his sword aimed straight at my belly, Ashlyn. I could not have handled both of them."

Ashlyn mumbled something that sounded like she was happy to oblige him, but her words were unintelligible. Aye, she was still struggling to calm herself. Braden brought the horses over, so Magnus led Ashlyn over to her horse and heaved her up onto the beast's back, not giving her the chance to argue about her ability to do it herself. He admired Ashlyn for her independence and her fierce streak, but this was not the time to be obstinate.

Fortunately, she apparently agreed with him because she didn't argue, just turned her horse back toward the ravine.

"Any other injuries to our men?" Magnus asked as he mounted his horse, his eye on Ashlyn. He feared she'd tumble off her horse in her present state, but she moved ahead of him, her back as straight as one of her arrows.

"Nay," Jamie said. "There were four guards not far away so they joined in as soon as they heard the shouts. I sent the rest off in search for a clearing. I believe there's a cave up ahead that will be a good place for us to sleep tonight. We should not be having this trouble at this time of year. Most of the reivers head south to escape the snow."

Braden returned Ashlyn's bow to her, and the four of them rode together.

"Ashlyn, you are hale?" Magnus asked after a moment.

"Aye." But he heard naught else from her.

The incident had shaken her for sure. Magnus lowered his voice, hoping Ashlyn wouldn't hear him, and said, "The bastard hit her in the face with his fist. She's likely to have a shining eye by morn."

"Ashlyn will deal with it. I don't like that they were able to get to her. We made an error in judgment. We need to discuss this when we're eating."

As they rode back, a sound overhead caught their attention, but Ashlyn reacted first, readying her bow and arrow and catching a duck that flew overhead. The bird's body landed next to Braden.

"Great. We've got our dinner," Braden grinned. "Wonder what the others will eat? Not many rabbits around this time of year."

A few more ducks followed the other in flight, so Ashlyn took another one out.

"Hellfire!" Braden said. "I'm glad you're with us, Ashlyn. I couldn't have hit them."

Braden retrieved both fowl and hooked them to his saddle as they traveled ahead, watching for signs of the others.

Braden pointed to a clearing off to the side of the main path. Horses were tied up outside a cave. Once they tied their horses to the bushes, they made their way into the shelter. The other four lads stood inside, arms crossed as if they were ready for an argument. Coll started to speak, but Magnus held up a hand to quiet him. He removed the two ducks from Braden's horse and held them up for all to see.

Coll's face lit up. "Och, Braden, nice aim! They'll make a tasty dinner tonight. I thought we were stuck with oatcakes."

Magnus walked up so his face was less that an arm's length from Coll's. "You can thank Ashlyn. She shot them both down, and this one is huge."

Coll clamped his mouth shut.

Once their meal was almost finished, they settled on a few logs arranged just inside the large cave. Jamie stood up and announced, "Ashlyn?"

She spun her head around to stare at her cousin, wondering what the hellfire he was about to say. Did he wish to send her back? She hesitated with bated breath.

Jamie said, "You need to plait your hair."

Her face fell. "I know. I'll have it plaited before we leave." She hoped that would end it. Much as she didn't wish to agree, she knew it was necessary for her own safety. One, she was easily identified as a lass. Two, her long hair had interfered with her vision.

"Who were they?" Jamie asked. "Anyone recognize them?"

They all denied having any direct knowledge of the attackers.

"I did not know them," Tormod said. "'Tis unusual to see a group of men without their plaid."

"They do not wish to be identified," Magnus said.

"Mayhap they are—or *were*—MacNiven's men," Ashlyn said. Seven faces turned to look at her.

"What?" She shrugged her shoulders. "He hides behind a helm to keep from being recognized. Aline said he went by MacNeil in Castle Dubh. It fits."

She did not like the way some of the men were casting sideways glances at her. Apparently, she was not the only one who noticed it.

"Problem?" Magnus asked, setting his hand on his thigh.

Ashlyn noticed how Magnus moved his hand closer to his sword whenever he wanted the others' attention. Silence filled the air as they finished their food.

"No problem, Magnus. Just a comment. They were after the

lass." Coll's eyes bored into hers. She could feel several sets of eyes on her, but none held as much fury as his did.

Tossing his last bone into the fire, Osgar said, "MacNiven's men or not, they might not have attacked us at all if not for Ashlyn. She is easily identified."

Jamie stood, moving closer to Osgar. "She'll be plaiting her hair on the morrow. Enough discussion on the hair."

"I'll be plaiting it for her tonight," Magnus added.

Jamie continued, "We need to focus on the fact that this could be MacNiven, which I'll remind you is our charge. On the morrow, we shall search for any signs of where they originated, possibly find a lead to where MacNiven may be. Unfortunately, there are none left to lead us to their chief. It may have been MacNiven, it may have been our usual reivers."

"Those men would have attacked anyone coming through the ravine. We were just the next ones through. They were after our horses. They noticed the lass and decided to take her, too." Magnus crossed his arms in front of him, eyeing each of the men in turn. She wondered what was going through his mind.

Jamie replied, "True, but I think we must investigate the possibility it was MacNiven. Anyone else agree with me?"

Ashlyn cleared her throat. "Aye, 'twas MacNiven's men. I heard them yell to go for the lass. Aunt Gwyneth was almost sold to someone in the East. Mayhap Ranulf MacNiven plans to sell lasses in the burgh to men who wish to own them. My guess is he's searching for another source of income now that Hew Gordon is dead. Though he has a substantial amount of gold from Gordon, he'll need more if he wishes to raise a force strong enough to attack the Ramsays or the Grants. This was his original mission, and I doubt he has given up on it, just changed his method. 'Tis anyone's guess as to where he shall go next."

"So you would have been sold outright?" Braden asked, his eyes wide.

"I believe so."

"Hellfire, we need to stop the bastard."

"Mayhap having a lass along interferes with our ability to find MacNiven," Art said.

"Or mayhap it will bring him to us. She could be our best asset." Jamie pursed his lips, a look she recognized all too well.

Her cousin was daring anyone to disagree with him. "And while we're discussing our group of guards, allow me to mention a couple of things. First is that Ashlyn took two of the eight men out before she was captured, one that had their sword aimed for my belly. Second thing is that I noticed one of our arrows endangered one of our own. I know not who shot it, but I know the direction it came from."

"What?" Tormod stood, and the rest of the group followed his lead. "Someone tried to shoot one of us?"

"One of the enemies held a bow," Osgar shouted. "It did not necessarily come from one of us."

Questions flew as they all took one another's measure. Dread slid down Ashlyn's spine. She'd hoped the attacks had ended after they'd left Clan Grant. Why would one of the men still be after her?

"Who was the target?"

"Who would do that?"

"Why would someone shoot a clanmate?"

Jamie put an end to the discussion. "I saw it, and it was aimed at Ashlyn. It didn't come from her protector or her family. The conversation ends here with this piece of advice. If you cannot handle traveling with a lass, go home now, and I'll not hold it against you. Do it again, and I'll see you dead when we leave you behind. Get some sleep. Ashlyn will be at the back of the cave, and Magnus and I will be in front of her." The threat was obvious in that last line.

As the others settled in, Magnus took Ashlyn by the arm and led her to the back of the cave. He settled her on a rock and stood behind her, weaving his fingers through her hair to straighten it as best he could.

"Magnus, I can plait my own hair. It just takes a while because 'tis so long."

"As I said, I plaited Rhona's hair all the time. I am quite skilled at it, and she used to say it relaxed her. After the day you've had, I think that sounds like a good idea." He spoke in a low voice, low enough so the others couldn't hear him as they rustled around in preparation for the night's rest.

Some of the men were speaking in hushed tones, and Ashlyn was quite pleased that she couldn't hear what they were saying. It would be a greater challenge to ignore Magnus's ministrations. His hands massaged her scalp as he pulled the strands apart. She stifled a moan as she leaned back into his hands.

Magnus chuckled, but said naught as he tamed the wild locks and then began his ritual of plaiting them, each touch to her scalp a sweet caress before he pulled the curls back, braiding carefully. She gave him complete control—something she had never willingly done before—leaning her neck and her body whichever way he wished.

Who would have thought such a simple touch could be so…stirring?

"Do not allow the men to upset you. The same happens to any man on his first venture." The soft tones of his voice soothed her almost as much as his fingers on her scalp.

"Did it happen to you?" She closed her eyes, giving in to the rhythmic pulls of his hands winding her hair together.

"Aye, one of my clanmates tried to suggest that I slowed them down because I am so large. He claimed I could not run fast and it would be a risk to have me along."

"What did you do?"

"I advised him to start running, then I chased him down in short order and put my fist in his face."

Ashlyn stifled her laughter with a hand over her mouth, leaning back into him even more. "Did it work?"

"Aye, he never bothered me again."

He continued his task without speaking, and it was just as well. Ashlyn suddenly found herself incapable of speech. The more hair he wound, the more sensitive she became. If her mouth opened, the only thing he would hear would be a sweet moan of pleasure. When Magnus finished, he tied a leather thong around the ends of her plaits, pulling them tight, and then leaned forward and whispered into her ear.

"Sweet dreams, lass."

She did not have to look at him to know how big the grin was on his face.

# CHAPTER SEVEN

While Ashlyn had thought Magnus's light snores would prove to be a bother, in fact, they seemed to lull her to sleep. It proved a source of comfort to know he was still there in the back of this deep, dark cave full of noisy male bodies. Ashlyn slept like a deer in the dark.

Jamie awakened them at dawn, and Ashlyn brushed the sleep from her eyes and made her way outside to relieve herself. When she returned, she was surprised to find the guards talking with Uncle Logan. "Greetings, lass. You took a fist in the face, I see."

Ashlyn reached up to touch her face, amazed to feel the swelling there. "Aye, I'm sorry. I'll get my things together. My face is of no concern." She glanced at Magnus in time to catch him assessing her injury, his usual smile replaced with a look of fury he hid a moment later. She pivoted to return to the back of the cave for her belongings but was stopped by her uncle. "Ashlyn, you feel confident they were MacNiven's men?"

"Aye. There was something about them, not the man who captured me, but one of them was familiar. 'Twas as if I'd heard his voice before." She paused as something fell into place in her mind. "In fact, I recall something from when I was face down on his horse. I didn't remember until just now. There was a trail off the path we followed."

Uncle Logan's face lit up. "A trail? And no one else noticed it? Who else was near you?"

"Myself, Jamie, and Braden," Magnus said. "I did not notice aught." He glanced at Jamie for his response.

"Nay, I saw naught. Where exactly, Ashlyn?"

"At the beginning. The leaves were spread out unnaturally, the way you showed me. It was like someone had covered something up. Our other lads were gathered by that spot."

The rest of the warriors exchanged looks before giving their attention to Logan. There was a chorus of nays and naughts—no one remembered seeing signs of a trail.

"I rode back to see if any of you had found a lead," Logan said. "If you think there was something there, Ashlyn, we'll go check."

"If no one else noticed it, it must be naught," Osgar growled, his color high. "She was face down on a horse. Saints above, if 'twas real, we would have all noticed it."

Uncle Logan's gaze narrowed on Osgar. "You are quick to discount a fellow warrior. Ashlyn, Magnus, and I will go check, and anyone else who wishes to follow along."

"I'll follow," Tormod said, nodding. "She has good sense."

"Aye," Coll agreed. "I shall come."

Art grumbled, "I'll wait here with Osgar."

Once they had their things together, everyone except Art and Osgar mounted up and rode back the way they had come. They didn't go back far before Ashlyn stopped her horse and held her hand up for the rest to stop. She dismounted and searched the area, a grin creeping across her face at the realization that it was just as she remembered. She pointed. "Here, Uncle Logan." She moved the leaves aside and found signs of horses.

Uncle Logan dismounted and made his way toward her. "Well done." He continued on foot, then announced, "Probably at least six horses. I'll lead the way."

They traveled single file until they came upon a cave. Uncle Logan dismounted, grabbing his sword and moving toward the mouth of the cave. Jamie and Braden followed directly behind him. He pointed to an area off to one side for Ashlyn and Magnus to go, and a place on the other side for the remaining men. Jake had told her it was good practice to have archers hidden and always ready to shoot.

A few moments later, the first group emerged from the cave. Uncle Logan was carrying a plaid. "They've gone," he said. "The fire is still warm. I think they were scared off after losing so many men. I cannot tell for certes if MacNiven was with them, but my hunch is that he was here. He may be moving south, just as we are. We'll find him. Search outside to see if you find aught before we take our leave."

As they spread out, an awful sound rent the air. An arrow flew past Ashlyn's head, missing by a hair, and bounced off the stones behind her. Uncle Logan returned fire faster than Ashlyn could nock an arrow. He shot three arrows before they heard the strangled scream of pain.

Magnus took off into the woods in the direction Uncle Logan had been shooting. They followed him, and Ashlyn stopped dead in her tracks when she came upon him.

Rage emanated from Magnus as he delivered blow after blow into Osgar's face, ignoring the arrows sticking out of the fool's belly and the bow and arrow at his feet, ignoring the fact that the man was almost certainly dead. "You shoot at a fellow Grant warrior? Bastard. I'll kill you with my bare hands if those arrows do not." It looked like that would not be necessary, but Ashlyn believed him.

Art rode in behind them on his horse. "Hellfire." He glanced down at Osgar. Uncle Logan and Jamie had pulled Magnus off the dead man. A bellow ripped out of him, but when he finally wrestled away from them, he took a step back, panting, and stood there with his fists clenched at his sides.

"Art, you are part of this?" Jamie asked.

Art's face turned pale. "Nay. He left, saying he had to relieve himself, but when he didn't return, I decided to see where he had gone. I knew he was upset about having a lass on our team, but I never thought he would go this far."

Magnus, still panting, whispered, "Ash, you are hale?"

Jamie turned to her, a stunned expression on his face. "Sorry, lass. We should have seen this coming."

"Nay," Uncle Logan barked. "How were you to predict that he would ambush his own clan? He turned traitor, not just on the lass, but on all of us. 'Tis good we discovered him before he could see his plan through." He walked up to Osgar's body and spat on him. "The buzzards for you." He mounted his horse and left, the rest followed—all but Magnus and Ashlyn.

Ashlyn glanced up at the giant warrior, her eyes misting. "Twice. 'Tis twice you've had to protect me on this journey. I must thank my uncle Alex." She could not speak any more or she would lose control of her emotions. Her excitement for the journey had blinded her to the dangers. She'd had no idea she would be the target of two different people, especially so early on. Mayhap she'd made a big mistake. She'd hoped to be an asset, not a detriment.

Magnus wrapped his hands around her waist and set her up on her horse. "Remember, 'tis not your fault. You were the only one to see the trail MacNiven's men tried to cover. I know 'twill be difficult, but you must put this behind you. We need you, Ashlyn."

Ashlyn nodded and tugged on the reins, guiding her horse forward.

When they finally made it back to the cave, Jamie said, "Ready yourself, Ashlyn. "We leave in ten minutes."

Uncle Logan mounted and said, "I'll see you in Edinburgh. I wish to scout on my own for a bit."

Ashlyn stared after he beloved uncle. How she wished she could be as strong as he was. She forced herself to finish her task and focus on what was in front of her.

None of them discussed the incident further, but it was clear to Ashlyn that Jamie had said something to the other warriors before she and Magnus had arrived. This was a matter of honor. She'd often heard her uncle Alex say that lads who battled together must trust one another.

This was no different.

Days later, they arrived in Edinburgh. Magnus had to admit the royal burgh set his stomach to churning, since he'd never been in such a place before. He'd spent all his days at Clan Grant or fighting for Clan Grant. True, they'd had minstrels and fairs and weddings at their festivals at Clan Grant, but this was so grand. It made him feel small in comparison. Of course, it was not only the city that unsettled him—he had to admit that his feelings toward Ashlyn were growing even stronger. After all the times he'd sworn he'd never fall for another, he did not like the way his heart yearned for her. The way she'd leaned in to him as he plaited her hair had made him want her—a frightening sensation for a man who'd sworn to shut himself off.

The loss of Rhona and his son had been almost unbearable. He'd felt abandoned, and though it shamed him to think about it, he'd even felt angry with his wife for deserting him. Aye, he knew it was not her fault, but he had felt so alone and desperate. Now he was used to being alone. He had his two dogs, his duties to his clanmates, and that was it. It had satisfied him enough a moon ago, why risk falling in love when he knew it could end in torture?

Nay, he was better off staying alone. He stopped his horse about the same time Tormod stopped his.

Tormod looked up at the royal castle atop the hill. "It looks as though it touches the heavens, does it not?" He turned to Magnus, a smile erupting on his face. "I've not seen it before. Have you?"

Magnus shook his head. "I've heard talk of it, but 'tis my first journey to Edinburgh. What a sight and what a castle. Though Grant Castle is almost the same size."

Jamie rode up to him from behind. "But the scrolls and ornate work are much different. You'll see when we arrive in their courtyard."

Magnus couldn't believe all the people in the burgh. Everywhere he looked there were people, and the streets were filled with vendors and food booths. Buildings lined both sides. They took a different road to the castle gates. Magnus glanced over at Ashlyn to see how she fared, and he followed her gaze to the top of the towers.

"What are you thinking, Ash?"

She blushed, something he did not see often from her. "I was wondering if there were any stories about the towers. 'Tis quite a beautiful castle, is it not?"

The guards opened the iron gate to allow them passage into the castle. They slowed their horses as they gazed at the wonder around them. Aye, Castle Grant was beautiful, but this was beyond belief.

Magnus whispered to Ashlyn, "Do you see below? 'Tis almost as if we are in the clouds. We are above the trees and the clouds look to be within our reach."

Ashlyn nodded, staring at the landscape of the burgh below them. "Look. The toths are all in nice rows below. You can see each merchant's booth and their home behind them. Even the banners and flags appear more majestic from here. 'Tis a lovely view."

There were only seven of them. Jamie had decided not to replace Osgar at such a late hour. He'd informed the extra guards of all that had transpired, giving them strict instructions to return to Grant land and report the news to his sire and brother. Due to the risk of heavy snow, he'd ordered the extra guards not to rejoin them—the risk of waiting was too steep—so their small group continued ahead into the mountains.

While they'd been warned about the possibility that snow would prevent their return, Magnus hoped they would get home. His dogs would be undone if he did not return before winter set in. He wondered how Ashlyn felt.

When they reached the royal castle, stable lads rushed forward to assist them, moving to Ashlyn's side, but Magnus sent them off to help the others. "I've got her, lads. Tend to the horses, take good care of them, they've had a long journey."

He caught Ashlyn by the waist, and he felt but did not hear her quick intake of breath. Was he actually getting through to her? He chided himself for his wishful thinking. His hands were probably cold from the dropping temperature and the winds, though he'd kept them covered for the most part. At least she was unlikely to notice his pleased grin, both because he was usually smiling and because her attention kept jumping to the others in the courtyard. Full of people bustling around, the castle attracted many in their finery. He wondered what roles many of them filled, but did not dare ask. Instead, he glanced out toward the horizon, taking a moment to enjoy the Scottish landscape in the burgh with its hills, valleys, pine trees, and ornate stone buildings.

As he slid Ashlyn down close to his body, he said, "Does this view make you wish to be snowed in here? Are you hoping to stay here until spring?"

"Nay!" she retorted. "I do not wish to spend my winter here. You do not think 'tis a true possibility, do you? I wish to go home within a fortnight." There was a thread of uncertainty, almost of fear, in her voice and gaze. Nay, she did not want to be away from home for the winter any more than he did.

"Lass," he said gently, "I know little about the weather here in Edinburgh, so I cannot advise you. But I also hope to return to the clan before the storms hit. Only time will inform us of the truth."

"Lads. Over here!" The voice was Logan Ramsay's. He stood in the courtyard, chatting with some of the king's guards. He had clearly arrived well ahead of them, and Magnus would guess he had not discovered any more about MacNiven than they had.

Jamie and Braden rushed up to Logan, and Ashlyn and Magnus followed with the others. As he crossed the grounds, Magnus took note of the number of castle guards posted around the periphery of the yard. There would be no attacking this castle. Set on the hill as it was, every traveler would be seen in advance. Whoever had designed it had done so brilliantly.

Logan ushered them inside the heavy castle doors and led the way to a chamber at the end of a long passageway. Magnus was transfixed by the swords and tapestries lining the walls, some of the weapons embedded with gemstones, and others quite old and dull. After they passed the great hall, an enormous space filled with people, Jamie turned to address them. "Uncle Logan prefers privacy for our meetings. The king usually accommodates him."

As soon as they entered the private chamber, Logan's wife Gwyneth rose from the table to greet them. This chamber was smaller than the great hall they had passed, but about the same size as the Grant hall. A large table sat in the center, and there were hearths along the outside wall. The chairs all had soft cushions, a luxury they did not possess at Clan Grant. Their hall held many trestle tables and benches to accommodate as many as possible. This chamber had clearly been designed for someone the king believed deserving of the best treatment. He glanced at Ashlyn, and the look on her face told him she was as humbled as he was to be in a castle of such riches. The table was set with silver goblets and fine needlepoint linen cloths.

Gwyneth introduced the lads to two of her daughters, Sorcha and Molly, who were also present. Coll, Art, and Tormod did their best to use their polite manners. Though the lads had seen Logan Ramsay and his wife visit Clan Grant before, they were far more familiar with Gwyneth Ramsay's reputation as a spy for the Crown and the top archer in all of England.

Magnus whispered to Ashlyn, "Your aunt is still a fine looking woman. Look at the lads drooling at her feet."

Ashlyn chuckled. "The best part about it is that it means naught to her. While some lasses would fall for their charms, Aunt Gwyneth is oblivious to all lads other than Uncle Logan. But Molly appears a bit more interested in the lads than I've seen her before."

"So she does." He gave a slight tip of his head in the direction of Molly, who had indeed settled her attentions on Coll, Art, and Tormod. Sorcha was joking with her cousins, Braden and Jamie. A few moments later, Molly came over to greet Ashlyn. They'd always gotten along well because they came from similar backgrounds. Like Ashlyn and Gracie, Molly and Maggie, her sister, had been adopted.

Uncle Logan finally waved his arms to indicate they should sit, while Aunt Gwyneth found serving maids to send for food and drink. When she returned, Uncle Logan closed the door and motioned for everyone's attention. Ashlyn sat at the trestle table between Molly and Magnus.

"I have news, but first I'd like to hear what happened to the eighth member of your party," Logan said. "Your sire told me he planned to send eight lads."

Gwyneth cleared her throat, giving her husband a pointed look.

Logan added, "Forgive me, Ashlyn. A *team* of eight. Wasn't that his intent? Were you not to replace Osgar with one of his periphery guards?"

"Aye," Jamie replied. "That was his original intent, but I decided to continue with the group we had. Seven is our total."

Logan nodded in approval. "You cannot have disagreement among your team." He gave Coll, Tormod, and Art pointed looks. "I know we discussed this before after Osgar showed his true colors, but I wish to ask again. The lot of you can accept females on your team? Because I have brought three more to help us. If you have an issue with it, speak now."

Ashlyn had to control her urge to break out in laughter. Would anyone here dare speak against Logan Ramsay? She did not know anyone who would, and certainly not the three who had come along. Judging from the looks on their faces, Coll, Art, and Tormod all looked quite willing to travel with the women who had just joined them.

"I will not make this long. As soon as you have refreshed yourselves, we will leave for Buchan land. King Alexander wants Ranulf MacNiven found, and we have agreed that MacNiven's old friend, Glenn of Buchan, must be consulted first. I believe we disrupted MacNiven's plans by killing many of his men back near the ravine. So my guess is he is searching out more men. Between the attack on Clan Grant and the ravine, he's lost many. He needs to regroup, and I believe he may be heading to Buchan land for assistance. Whether he gets help or not from Glenn is yet to be seen. But since neither of us uncovered any more about him, I'd like to question Glenn of Buchan.

"There are eleven of us. The king's guards will accompany us to ensure Buchan allows us entry. On my last visit, he refused to see me, but this time his refusal will not be accepted. Once inside, we will be on our own, and I plan to split into two teams. We must discover MacNiven's whereabouts, but first I wish to determine if Glenn is part of his scheme."

A knock on the door announced the arrival of servants bearing dishes of stew, carrots, and bread.

"Be ready to leave in two hours," Uncle Logan said. "For those of you that are new to Edinburgh, you many wander around after we return. Please stay on the royal grounds until then."

Once Uncle Logan sat down, the dishes made their way around the table.

Molly leaned over to Ashlyn and whispered, "Tell me about Tormod. He's cute."

Just before nightfall, they arrived at the Buchan keep, several of the king's guards flanking their own. Ashlyn's gut could not unclench—the thought that she was actually riding alongside her uncle Logan was enough to undo her. Now that the groups had combined, they would be called the Ramsay and Grant guards.

Magnus and Jamie approached the gate and spoke to the five guards directly behind the portcullis. "Logan Ramsay here on the king's order for Glenn of Buchan."

She thought the gates would open, but they did not. A few of the horses started prancing as if sensing the tension in the air. Was this how it felt just before a skirmish? She fingered her bow, making sure she could move it quickly if the need arose.

"Ramsays are not allowed in without the chief's permission," the guard grumbled.

"Then it's the Grant guards here on King Alexander's order." Uncle Logan ran his horse up to the gate, making sure the guards could see how ready he was to do battle.

"We've sent for the chief. You must wait for his permission to allow you inside."

"Fine," Uncle Logan barked. "Tell him to get his arse out here. Logan Ramsay and Ranulf MacNiven wish to see him."

Magnus turned his head to glance at Ashlyn, his brow raised, his mouth tipped up in its habitual smile. Molly, whose horse was on Ashlyn's other side, whispered, "That should be enough to get the Buchan out here."

A few moments later, the portcullis raised and Glenn of Buchan rode out to greet them, escorted by another five of his guards. He headed straight for Logan Ramsay. "As a participant in the murder of both of my sons, you are not welcome here. Take your group off my land at once, Ramsay."

"I have a writ from the king. I'm here on his orders. 'Twould be treasonous for me to ignore them, but then you are quite familiar with treason, are you not?" Logan's gaze narrowed as he spoke to the Buchan. Anyone within shouting distance could see the hatred between the two men. "I'll have the guard bring it forward to read it to you."

"I prefer to hear about MacNiven first. I assume he is not actually here with you?"

"As you wish. Nay, he is not here, but Ranulf MacNiven is alive and well. He was last seen in the Highlands, where he attempted to start his own clan of warriors under the name MacNeil. The Grants ran him off. What do you know of this?"

"You are totally inappropriate, Ramsay. Ranulf MacNiven was hung for his actions, but you know that. Take yourself away."

Uncle Logan moved his horse close to Glenn. "I'm telling you I have seen the man with my own eyes. Ranulf MacNiven is alive and living in the Highlands, though after the Grants unmasked him, he has gone back into hiding. The king wishes to know your involvement in this treasonous act."

Ashlyn could see the shock that registered across Glenn of Buchan's features before he covered them. He cleared his throat and nodded, "You're allowed in, but only until this matter is settled. I wish to know more about this travesty. If he's alive, you are not the only one who desires revenge. He wronged my daughter."

The Buchan raised his arm, indicating that they be allowed to pass inside the gates. Logan said, "The king's guards are to wait outside the gate until I send them on."

"Suit yourself. Your group is welcome in my hall only. Do not be wandering around my bailey."

Logan nodded. "Agreed. Lead the way."

They led the horses, two abreast, into the bailey while some of Buchan's clanmates spat on the ground next to them. After making sure that all noted his clansmen's insults, Buchan ordered them to cease their disrespect.

The group found their way inside into the great hall in silence after leaving the stables. Buchan led them to a table where the guards were finishing their evening meal and loading up on ale. Once they settled and the chief ordered more food and ale, Buchan turned to his guests. "Tell me your news of MacNiven. Have you any proof that he lives?"

"He was seen in the Highlands," Logan replied. "If you wish, I'll bring the witnesses into your solar. I'll not discuss it out here amongst your guards."

The Buchan stood and pointed to his solar off the great hall. Uncle Logan motioned for Magnus, Jamie, and Ashlyn to follow him. Ashlyn stood, and Jamie moved to grab her arm as if he'd noticed her shaking legs.

To her own surprise, she allowed it. This place assailed her with bitter memories of Ayrshire. Everywhere she looked, there were angry faces and domineering males. She was grateful to have Jamie on one side and Magnus on the other. Halfway across the huge hall, Magnus placed his hand against the small of her back, using his bulk to help hide her from the stares of all the men in the room.

He'd made the move as smoothly as possible, as if he'd sensed what was inside her. It was exactly the support she needed, and in fact, she found herself grabbing his left hand with hers. Her skin crawled as if covered in insects, and the leering sneers of several of the guards making her feel dirty, unkempt, and ready to heave into the nearest corner. Maybe she should have stayed home. The creeping sensation across her neck told her Gracie had been right all along: she ought not have left Clan Grant.

Men, there were men everywhere—ugly, dirty, ogling, smirking men.

"You'll regret it," her sister had whispered the day she'd left.

*Nay, Gracie, I'm stronger than that. They cannot break me with a look. I matter. I am important.*

Propelled back in time, she found herself hiding behind a familiar outcropping of rocks as a horrible man beat her mother, hitting her beautiful face with his fists. Ashlyn had covered her ears to stop her mother's screams, but she could still hear them. The Norsemen on the galley ship were hooting and hollering about her mother, spouting filth in a foreign language that did nothing to disguise their meaning. She checked on Gracie, but her wee sister still lay sound asleep on the soft ground under the tree.

But not Ashlyn, nay. Her senses on alert, the whole environment changed on her in a second. In the middle of the night, another Norseman had come. The touch, she felt the touch, and she screamed, grabbing her dagger. His hand went for Gracie's tender skin, and she swung with all her might. She swung and swung and swung. *Get away, get away, leave us be. You cannot touch her. You cannot touch me. Leave us.* Then the absolute worst happened, the one thing she had tried so hard to erase from her memory.

Magnus pinched the skin on her arm and she gasped as she spun her head to face him. The other man disappeared in an instant, replaced with this beautiful man who was her protector. What had happened? Magnus had pulled her from her nightmare, the vortex that had engulfed her on so many nights and even days. She swiped at the tears on one cheek, hoping that Jamie hadn't seen them. Magnus leaned over and brushed his shoulder against her other cheek, soaking her tears up with his plaid, doing his best to hide her sadness from the others.

Uncle Logan and Glenn entered the solar, trailed by Buchan's two guards. Jamie stepped in front of Ashlyn as Magnus fell in behind her, the two of them cocooning her as they entered the room. She willed her strength to prevail.

*You can be strong, sweet one. Lassies can be strong just like laddies.* It was her sire's voice, pulled from distant, beloved memories, and she felt her strength grow and grow in her chest.

Uncle Logan fell in beside her in an attempt to hide her weak state, but the Buchan noticed and shoved him aside.

"Och, what have we here? A weak ninny you brought with you, Ramsay?" A malicious grin covered his face.

But that grin disappeared as soon as Magnus grabbed him and lifted him so high over his head that he almost touched the ceiling. Buchan's guards had their swords aimed at Magnus's chest, ready to spill blood at a nod from their chief.

"You'll be dead in an instant if you do not release me," Glenn rasped.

# CHAPTER EIGHT

Magnus's voice, deep and menacing, echoed in the chamber. "Apologize to the lass for your disrespect. You must teach your guards better manners. I saw the way they were leering at her in the hall."

Logan's hand moved to Magnus's arm. "Let him down, Magnus. We know Ashlyn's value. The scum in this hall mean naught to her, am I not correct, Ashlyn?"

Squaring her shoulders, Ashlyn lifted her chin and said, "They mean naught to me, Magnus. You may release him."

He felt the touch of her hand on his shoulder, so he lessened his grip, but he held the Buchan chief up so they were eye-to-eye. "You'll not disrespect her," he ground out. He'd kill the bastard with his bare hands, chieftain or not. He would not allow this pile of lard to distress Ashlyn any longer. He'd noticed her drift into another world as they'd continued through the hall, unable to ignore all the insulting, degrading looks from the guards. Alex Grant would never allow such behavior in his hall. This fool had no honor, none at all.

But he could not risk the lives of the others. He took a deep breath and lowered the weasel slowly. When he set the Buchan down, the chieftain's guards finally stood back, returning their swords to their sides.

The Buchan laughed as he took a seat behind his desk. "Was that not entertaining? All over a lass. Why do you not take seats so we can dispense with our business and you can be on your way?"

Once they were seated, he continued, "As far as MacNiven's concerned, I am certain whatever you've heard is utter nonsense. He was hung for treason as the king ordered. While my daughter wishes for him to still be alive, enough to have affected her sound reasoning, I know he was hanged as ordered. 'Tis foolish to try to convince me of aught but the truth."

Logan said, "I have three witnesses here who can attest to the fact that he is very much alive."

"I'd like to know how these witnesses are certain the lad they saw is MacNiven. If he is still alive, and I say *if*, then he would return to marry Davina. Even though she was meant to marry your nephew, Ramsay, MacNiven had plans to marry my daughter eventually. He adored her."

"I have seen him from a distance, but my nephew Jake, who met him at my family keep, said he came face to face with him, no helm. He called him by his true name, and Ranulf was upset he'd been recognized."

"Why would he be in the Highlands?"

The confusion on Buchan's face made Magnus believe he told the truth. The chief did not believe that MacNiven had escaped the hangman's noose. Magnus had also heard that at the king's castle, Davina had admitted to being forced into marrying Torrian, and that Ranulf planned to take over the Ramsay clan. Hadn't that been his plan before he changed to the takeover of the Highlands and the Grants? Hadn't he heard something about Ranulf ridding the world of Torrian, something Lily had overheard him say?

There was much gossip about the entire travesty, and he knew not which story he should believe. But it did unsettle him that Buchan was not aware that MacNiven lived.

"He planned to take over the Highlands, but the Grants foiled his plans in less than a day. Clearly, you know his reasons for heading to the Highlands. If he had been discovered anywhere near Edinburgh, he would have been caught and hung."

Buchan stared at Logan, processing all he'd heard.

Ashlyn spoke up. "I saw him in the kitchens up close."

"And how in hell would you recognize him? I've not seen you before." His cold eyes bore into hers, testing her. "You're lying, and there's naught you can say to make me believe 'tis true."

"You are correct. I had never seen him before the skirmish in the Highlands. But I can tell you what I observed of the man who was driving the attack on the Grants." Ashlyn stood her ground and whispered, "He has two scars. One below his left cheek…"

Buchan jumped out of his chair, his hands on the desk. "You lie…"

"And a circular one on his right hand, near his thumb."

Magnus had never seen a person change from red to white so fast. Buchan paled and fell back in his chair, the next moment crossing himself and asking for God's blessing. He was not acting. Buchan had no idea that MacNiven had escaped the noose.

As soon as he regained his senses, he stared at Logan. "I want him. Bring him to me."

Logan smirked and crossed his arms. "That could be a problem. We have not seen him since the last battle. He found a bag of coins and left the area. He could have been killed and his body eaten by a wild animal or…"

"Or?" The Buchan stood up again, kneading his hands in front of him. "Or what?"

Logan stood and the rest followed. "Or he's still alive and in hiding until spring, when the snow ends."

Jamie added, "Are you claiming you knew naught of this? You were not involved in a plot to send him to fight my clan?"

Magnus could not believe Jamie pushed the man even more. He was learning much about warring tactics.

Buchan's face contorted in rage again. "Nay, I had naught to do with it. I had no idea he had escaped his own hanging. How the hell did he do it? Besides, my revenge is against the Ramsays, not the Grants."

"Some think Ramsays and the Grants are the same," Magnus said.

"I do not. I *know* who killed my sons—both of them. 'Twas bad enough you robbed me of my firstborn son, Dugald, but less than a year later you killed Cormag. Dugald was mad, but Cormag was just a lad." His finger pointed to Logan's face. "And I hold your clan responsible. You will pay."

Logan chuckled and leaned toward Buchan. "'Twas that thinking that got MacNiven in trouble. 'Twill do the same for you. But you tell lies. You are as angry with the Grants as the Ramsays. Admit the truth for once."

"I said I'd forgive Dugald's death, but not Cormag's."

"Cormag denounced his clan. He came to me in Edinburgh asking for an escort to a new clan. He wanted naught to do with you. You ruined that relationship. And he was as daft as Dugald. The lad tried to steal my niece, Lily!"

Buchan exploded. "You want me to extend my anger to the Grants? That I can do. Take your Ramsays and your Grants off my land. We'll see who has the final say in this matter. Lies, all lies. You and yours will pay."

Ashlyn took a step back and ran directly into Magnus's chest. For some reason, she chose not to push away from him. Her body felt so soft and warm against him, and he wanted naught more than to protect her. Glenn of Buchan looked daft himself, so Magnus gripped Ashlyn's waist and tugged her closer. He did not trust this man in front of him.

She leaned against him.

Logan took another step forward and stood nose to nose with Buchan. "You are the one who is guilty of lying. You knew the king executed the wrong man, and you sent men to MacNiven in the north to help him attack the Grants, did you not? You'll be held accountable for your crimes before we're finished. And I think you know where he's hiding, too. Where is he?"

"I do not know where he is," Buchan insisted. "And I did not know he was still alive until you told me. I've been grieving the loss of my two sons. My daughter's almost daft from grief. Now get out. Take your guards and get off my land. Tell the king I know naught of MacNiven, but I want to know when you find him. He owes me just as do you. And both of you will pay!" The Buchan stormed out of his own solar, his guards following fast behind him.

The four of them waited a moment before starting their conversation. Jamie was the first to speak. "Do you believe him, Uncle? He seemed quite convincing."

Logan settled his hands on his hips. "I think he's telling the truth. If I were MacNiven, I do not know if I would have trusted Buchan. The man's suffered too many losses, too recently. He's emotional, as you can see. Emotion can cloud judgment. Nay, MacNiven found someone else to send him guards. I still think he's alive. Well done, Ashlyn. The scars you noticed convinced Buchan that the chieftain who attacked the Grants was indeed MacNiven. Unfortunately, we are no further along than we were before. Where the hell did the Buchan go?"

"I do not know," Magnus said, "but I need to find a garderobe."

"Take Ashlyn with you." Logan pointed to the door. "Go now. We'll be leaving soon. Ashlyn, take care of your needs because we will not be staying."

Jamie came with Magnus and Ashlyn, and the others returned to the hall. After Magnus and Ashlyn finished, they waited while Jamie took care of his needs. A small voice called to them from down the passageway, but the speaker was too far away for Magnus to make out the words. He and Ashlyn exchanged a look and then crept in that direction, moving away from the hall. They found a beautiful lass hiding in an alcove. Her hair was dark and fell in soft waves all down her back. Dressed in the finest of gowns, her eyes darted everywhere, as if she did not trust them. She had a regal presence, especially garbed in red velvet and golden threading. The twisting of her hands in her skirts told them much about her composure.

Jamie found them moments later, and his eyes glinted with recognition when he saw the lass. "Greetings, my lady. Ashlyn and Magnus, this is Davina of Buchan, the chieftain's daughter."

"Listen to me," Davina said. "My sire told me why you are here, and I want you to know something. I know it to be true." Her voice shook and her eyes darted up and down the passageway as she spoke. "Ranulf is alive. I've told my father, but he refuses to believe me."

"How do you know this?" Jamie asked.

"Because I saw him." She glanced down the passageway again. "Not him, but the man who was in his cell."

Magnus sputtered. "What are you talking about? Do not speak in riddles."

She waved her hand as if to dismiss Magnus. "I went to visit Ranulf before he was to hang. I loved him and he loved me, and I wished to say farewell to him. But the man in his cell…it was not Ranulf sitting there. The man just stared at me and said naught."

Jamie's arms flew out to his sides, his frustration obvious. "And you did not tell this to anyone?"

"Nay." She shook her head and tears formed on her lashes. "Nay, I could not. I loved him. The only person I told was Da and he insisted I was daft with grief. But I was not. I know what I saw, and the man in that cell was not Ranulf."

"Have you seen him since then, Davina?"

"Nay. But I often feel as though he is watching me." The lass's eyes looked haunted. A look Magnus recognized from men who'd suffered in battle, ones who constantly looked over their shoulder for the enemy.

Ashlyn asked, "Have you sensed him recently?"

"Not now, but I did a sennight ago. I swear he was here, but now he is gone. Please find him." She disappeared down the corridor.

They filled Logan in on their encounter with Davina when they returned to the great hall, then they ate a quick repast and left.

"We'll do some searching in Edinburgh," Logan said. "I do not think we'll find him here."

They made it back to the royal castle in the middle of the night. The women slept in one chamber and the men in another. Ashlyn was so tired, she wished to climb into bed in her gown, but she changed. Her aunts and cousins were all already asleep, and she stifled a yawn as she started to climb into the bed. Then she thought of something to tell Magnus, who was keeping watch in the hall, and she rushed over to the door and flung it open. She hadn't properly thanked him for standing up for her against Glenn of Buchan. He could have been stabbed, yet he had not backed down.

"What the hell?" Magnus sat up. At first he looked alarmed, but as soon as he determined she was in her night rail, he smiled, running his gaze up and down her body.

Forgetting her intent, she reacted to his perusal. "Stop that. I am not a piece of meat."

"Nay, you most certainly are not." He gave her his biggest smile and said, "Do you miss me already?"

She slammed the door in his face, though she could hear his chuckle on the other side. What had she been thinking? Hellfire, but she'd thank him on the morrow. He was too glib at the moment.

Slud, but he was right. She'd gotten quite accustomed to having him nearby, and she did not mind one bit that he was sleeping outside her door. She climbed into bed, trying her best not to bother her aunt or cousins. To her alarm, she could not stop thinking about the brute. True, he was not as handsome as her male cousins, but he was pleasing to her eyes, especially with that ridiculous smile on his face all the time. It was a comfort knowing he was nearby, and she fell asleep without feeling the slightest bit worried about the creatures of the night.

Magnus would protect her.

They slept in late the following day, and in the morn they agreed to travel through the burgh after dark to see what they could discover. After their late-day meal, Uncle Logan led them to one side of the courtyard. "Here are your assignments. Coll and Art will travel with me and my family. Tormod, you shall go with Ashlyn, Magnus, and Braden. Jamie will lead. My team will travel to the docks to see if we can learn aught about anyone selling women into slavery since this has happened before in the burgh. If you are not aware, Gwyneth and I have experience in this area, which is why I chose that duty for our team. Jamie, you are to take your team into the middle of the burgh to visit some inns and see if you can find any loose tongues in the taverns. If MacNiven is still operating, as we suspect, he must be seeking reinforcements. He lost many in the battle with the Grants at Castle Dubh. See if you can learn aught about that. We meet back here at midnight. If you need help, send someone back and we shall join you. Any questions?"

Ashlyn's heart beat so fast, she guessed they could see it through her mantle. She took in a couple of deep breaths to slow herself down. They had to find MacNiven—no other resolution was acceptable. Before they left, Logan gave them his last piece of advice that echoed Ashlyn's thoughts: "Find the bastard."

Just before they headed out the gates, Jamie turned to face his group. "We're splitting up so we can cover more ground."

"I agree," Magnus said, nodding. "Five traveling together is unusual."

"Tormod, once we get to the center of the burgh, you will join Magnus and Ashlyn," Jamie continued. "Braden and I will go off on our own." When they reached the center, an active area with tall buildings made of stone on either side of the narrow cobblestone street, Jamie pointed down the road. "I see three inns. We shall go to the first one. Magnus, you go check the area around the far one, then we can meet in the middle and plan our next move."

They separated, and Ashlyn's party made their way to the inn

Jamie had assigned to them. Tormod stood on one side of her, and
Magnus stood on the other. The closer they got to their destination,
the more people they ran into. A couple of minstrels were playing
in the middle of the road, attracting the attention of the passersby,
many of whom showed evidence of being intoxicated.

Ashlyn listened to conversations as she pushed her way through
the crowd. People spoke openly when they did not realize others
were listening. She stopped in the middle, turning toward Magnus.
"Why do we not just keep wandering through to pick up what
people are talking about?"

Magnus turned to Tormod. "We'll just eavesdrop for a bit, see
what we learn." He pointed off toward one direction. "You go that
way, and Ashlyn and I will go in this direction. We'll meet you
back at this spot."

They separated, and Ashlyn moved into the middle of a group,
staring at one of the minstrels. She picked up on several different
conversations:

"Have you found a lass to warm your bed tonight?"

"Nay, I'll go home to my wife."

"What do you think the king will have for a meal on the
morrow?"

She moved steadily through the crowd, Magnus not far from
her, hoping to overhear something to do with MacNiven.

"My sire says a storm is coming. He could tell by the squirrels."

"Let's go to the inn and see what we can find."

Ashlyn looked up and noticed Magnus's tall figure behind her.
Easing her way toward him, she asked, "Have you heard aught,
Magnus?"

"Nay. Only who is bedding whom later."

Off to the side, but still attached to the crowd, three men were
whispering to one another. She thought that odd since most of the
men at the inn were loudly boasting about their accomplishments.
"Over there, I'd like to hear what they are discussing."

They moved through the crowd until they stood not far away.

"I cannot hear a word they are saying," Magnus said, "and I do
not wish to move closer or we shall be suspect."

"Hush. I can hear them." She focused her attention on the three
lads near them, edging her way closer, but making sure not to
move too far away from Magnus.

The first one said, "This could be a good opportunity."

"Will it be enough to pay for a strumpet?"

"Nay, 'tis not a temporary thing. The man's called Chief Dubh, and he is looking for guards. He's paying top coin."

The men headed off in a different direction.

Ashlyn elbowed Magnus.

"What?" he whispered.

"Chief Dubh. They are talking about someone called Chief Dubh."

Ashlyn moved to follow them, but Magnus pulled her back. "Where are you going?"

"To follow them." She stared into his eyes, her gaze unwavering. "Chief Dubh must be MacNiven."

"I thought he went by MacNeil?"

"Who else could it be? Follow me. We are losing them."

"Nay, they are leaving the inn. We'll not follow them. 'Tis too dangerous, and we agreed to meet with Jamie shortly."

"Magnus! It could be our only chance." The people around them gave her looks—some wary, some curious. She hadn't meant to draw their attention, but the sense of urgency in her belly drove her.

Magnus quirked his brow at her, and all she could do was glower at him in return. "Why must you ruin this? 'Tis too late now." The men had disappeared completely. She searched the area, finally accepting that they had lost them.

"Our instructions were to go to the inns, or have you forgotten? We've wandered the area long enough. 'Tis time to do as we were told. As a warrior, you must do as your chief instructs you. One does not go off on their own." He tugged her back through the crowd, making his way toward Tormod.

"What have you learned, Tormod?" Magnus asked, his hand on the small of Ashlyn's back. It felt as if it belonged there, but she shot him a frown.

"I just heard talk of a Chief Dubh hiring men," Tormod responded.

Ashlyn jerked in response. "We heard the same. How do we find him?"

"They said they were waiting for more information. Apparently, he is asking for many men. 'Tis all I know." His hands settled on his hips as he scanned the area.

"Shall we go into the inn as instructed by Jamie?" Magnus asked.

Ashlyn led the way to the farthest inn, refusing to look at Magnus. Why did he insist on being so stubborn? As they neared the inn, Tormod pulled Magnus aside. "What shall we do with her when we go into the tavern?" she heard him say in an undertone.

Magnus shook his head. "She goes with us."

"They do not allow lasses into the taverns. Only the ones who work."

"No matter, she'll go in with us. I'll not leave her out on her own. Or did you have another idea?"

"Nay, unless you wish to sit outside with her," Tormod said, glancing at Ashlyn.

Magnus stepped past him and opened the door to the tavern, holding it for Ashlyn. Hellfire, she wished to be angry with him, but how could she? He was always there for her, supporting her, watching over her, or assisting her.

There was no time to stew over it, though, for the inn was full of patrons, many of whom seemed to be having a grand time with the serving girls. One in particular was quite bawdy, and she teased every man she walked past. Magnus found them a table in the corner and sent Tormod to the counter for three drinks.

Much as she tried, she heard naught. The conversations were dull, but very bawdy. One particular comment had her shaking her head and glancing at Magnus. "That wench has the best arse I've ever seen," the lad had said about the woman bringing drinks to the patrons. "I'd love to plow her tonight. Do you think she'll have me?"

Magnus stifled a guffaw while she narrowed her gaze at him. "Truly, men are such simpletons."

Magnus glanced at Tormod, who had just returned with their drinks. "Aye, but she does have a nice arse. What do you think, Tormod?"

Tormod stared at him wide-eyed, apparently afraid to discuss the topic in front of her. She jumped out of her seat. "I think 'tis time to go to the next inn."

"Lass, I'd like to finish my drink." Magnus chugged down half his ale as he followed her with his gaze. "But if you're eager to go, we'll follow you. There's naught for us here."

Moments later, they were all outside. Ashlyn tried to push away from them, but Magnus reached out and touched her arm. Speaking in an undertone, he said, "Forgive me, lass. I should not have been so crude with you, but I was trying to fit in with the crowd."

Tormod stepped in front of Ashlyn, keeping her between him and Magnus as he led the way to the next tavern. It was a protective move, but Ashlyn found she did not wish to object. The next tavern was more unruly than the last.

"Och," Tormod said, "they are more sotted than the last group. Mayhap their tongues will be looser."

They found a table in the corner since Jamie was not here yet, and Magnus ushered her into the seat closest to the wall, undoubtedly so he could continue to protect her. Once they all had drinks in front of them, she surveyed the lads in the inn.

One group was especially raucous, and Magnus turned his focus on them.

Ashlyn followed his gaze, but was distracted by a conversation she heard off to the left.

"We need to find young girls," a fair-haired lad said. Ashlyn's gaze shot to Magnus, but he and Tormod were deep in conversation, shooting occasional glances at the table that had originally caught Magnus's attention. They were oblivious to what was unfolding beside them.

"But why? I thought he was searching for guards," the lad's companion growled.

"Because, fool, they always want young girls. At least, most chiefs want some wenches along. If we find some willing…"

His friend guffawed. "Willing?"

"Aye, you get my meaning. If we bring one or two along, that could get us in as guards. Now finish your ale so we can find us a couple of wenches." He took a long swig of his ale.

"Ashlyn, we are not staying here long." Magnus knocked her elbow to draw her attention.

"Why not? Is there a problem?" She wanted to return her attention to the lads. Surely the fair-haired lad could lead them to MacNiven.

"Because I do not like the way these men are staring at you."

"I'll circle the chamber before we leave," Tormod said, jumping to his feet. "At least then we will have completed our assignment." He left without waiting to hear what Magnus thought about that.

Ashlyn looked around the room. A few lads were staring at her, but not many. What was Magnus's problem? She gave up and returned her attention to the two who had been discussing their search for young wenches.

They were gone.

"Nay!" She stood up from her stool, her eyes searching the tavern. "Where are they?"

"Who?" Magnus asked.

"The two men seated at that table," she whispered. She gave a slight nod to the table where the two lads had been sitting.

"They must have left. Why?"

"We must follow them," she urged. "I overheard them talking about stealing young wenches." She moved toward the door, only to find a human wall in front of her.

"Wait, please. Do not go out alone. I must tell Tormod before we leave." She tapped her foot as she waited for him. As soon as Magnus spoke to the other guard, she hurried out the door, hoping she would be able to locate them. Magnus followed directly behind her. She halted in the middle of the path, but then moved close to him to whisper.

"Where are they? Magnus, help me find them! They could lead us to MacNiven." She headed down the path just as Tormod burst out of the inn.

The very instant Magnus turned around to explain why they'd needed to leave in such a hurry, Ashlyn heard the word "chief" coming from around the corner of the next building. She ran ahead while Magnus and Tormod were wrapped up in their conversation, which was starting to sound like an argument.

As soon as she stepped around the corner, a fist caught her in the side of her head, knocking her out.

# CHAPTER NINE

Magnus said, "I'll not continue to argue with you, Tormod. Ashlyn says she overheard something, and I believe her."

He turned back toward her and his gut clenched. Where the hell was she? "Ashlyn?" He ran toward the corner of the building, which was where he'd last seen her, Tormod at his side.

When they turned the corner, Magnus heard a noise and looked at Tormod just in time to see him crumple to the ground after being hit in the head. The next instant, Magnus's head exploded in pain, and his world went dark.

When he awakened, he was in a dark chamber below ground, his hands tied behind him. Where was he? Where were Ashlyn and Tormod? There was a gag in his mouth, so he could not yell either. It was so dark, he had to wait until his eyesight adjusted before he could see aught else in the chamber.

Where was Tormod? Hellfire, but he'd done something stupid. He should never have taken his gaze off the lass. He and Tormod had caused this by disagreeing in a crowd. They'd made themselves easy targets.

The next thought that registered was that some lad had touched Ashlyn. He almost wished they'd knocked her out first. He tugged on the bindings around his wrists and smiled. The fools hadn't tied him nearly tight enough. It would take him a few minutes, but he'd be free of his bindings in no time.

While he worked on the ties around his wrists, he said a quick prayer that Ashlyn was strong enough to handle herself until he could get to her. He'd find her, but she had to hold her own for a bit. Something told him she would. Alex Grant and Logan Ramsay would never have agreed to include her on this mission if they'd doubted her abilities. Besides, he'd seen plenty of evidence of her strength.

*Hang on, Ash. I'm coming for you.*

He finally freed himself. After he'd dispensed with the ropes that had secured him, he glanced around him only to discover he was in a low chamber with a barricaded door. Though he threw himself at the door over and over, it showed no sign of yielding.

The thought of someone touching Ashlyn drove him onward. The fifth time he hit the door, he heard a crack in the wood, so he went at it a sixth time, releasing a bellow that would scare the daylights out of any bairn. Still, it didn't move.

But he'd attracted someone. A sound came from the outside. Magnus reached for his sword, an instinctive reaction, but of course, it was not in its sheath. Cursing, he punched the door with his fist. "Come on in and fight me, you bastard."

The door opened and a thin lad came straight at him with a sword, so Magnus sidestepped him, then lunged after him, knocking the sword out of his hand and tossing him against the far wall. The lad slumped to the floor, but Magnus needed to be sure he wouldn't follow him, so he picked him up and punched him square in his jaw, knocking him out. He grabbed the sword—*his* sword, he realized—and sheathed it.

Then an awful sound assailed his ears.

"You bitch. I'll kill you for that." Loud words from a very deep voice.

Ashlyn.

Slud, but her head hurt. When Ashlyn came to, she found herself in a chamber she'd never seen before. Two men sat at a table in the corner, the same ones she'd seen in the inn, drinking ale and discussing their plans. She closed her eyes and listened. She was lying on a pallet with her hands and feet bound and a piece of cloth stuffed in her mouth, so there would be no ready escape. Magnus and Jamie would come for her, but that would take time. She might as well learn all she could.

"I did not think you were serious about taking a wench with us."

"She's the one who was watching us at the inn," the fair-haired lad said. "We'll bring her to the meet at the crossroads tomorrow. Maybe she'll up our chances of getting work."

"I just wish to become a guard and earn some coin. I would rather not drag a feisty wench along."

"Think of her as a sort of gift for Chief Dubh."

"Who is he, anyway? I've not heard of him before the other day."

"I doubt we'll ever know his true identity. They say he always wears a helm or a mask. Mayhap his face is severely scarred. 'Tis not important. We only need to join him for a fortnight or so, earn our coin, and come back wealthy."

"When are we moving her, and what are we to do with the fool below? Why did you bring him here?"

"Because he was too big to hide anywhere," the fair-haired man scoffed. "Once we got him in the cart, it was easy to move him. Can we not sell him? He'd be a great guard for the chief."

"If you could get him to follow your orders, which I doubt. We'll just leave the man behind, he'll die after a few days with no food or water."

Ashlyn said a quick prayer that Tormod had gotten a message to Jamie and the others. Her captors could only be speaking of Magnus—and how it hurt to think of him suffering for her foolishness—but her clan would find them for sure.

She had to believe it. A loud banging sound interrupted the lads' talk.

"Shite. He must be awake down below."

"Go knock him out again. We cannot have him carrying on like that. He'll break down the door."

Ashlyn peeked through her lashes as the one lad took off through the door, grabbing a sword on his way out. The other lout looked down at her.

He sauntered over. "I think you are awake, lass. Your breathing has changed." He poked her arm.

*Do not touch me. Do not touch me. Do not touch me.*

He touched her again, his hand moving down her arm before coming to rest on her hip. "You have the kind of shape I like, something to hang on to. I do not like reed thin lassies who lack any soft flesh." He squeezed her hip and she bucked despite herself.

He was touching her; she had to get away. Her eyes flew open and she searched the chamber for anything she could use as a weapon. There was naught. She did her best to yell with the gag in her mouth, but no sound came out. His hand came up to squeeze her breast, and she jerked, trying to pull away from him, but he held on tight.

"Verra nice tits."

His smirk made her want to vomit, and her breath started to come out in anxious pants because she was losing control. She had to deal with this. Had to. Closing her eyes, she thought of Magnus and how tender and protective his touch had been in Buchan's solar. Her breathing slowed, and her mind felt sharper, clearer. Suddenly, an idea came to her.

She swung her knee up as hard as she could and caught her captor square in his ballocks.

He grabbed his male parts and bent over at the waist, yelling, "You bitch. I'll kill you for that."

The sound of running footsteps met her ears right before the door crashed open. Out of the corner of her eye, she saw Magnus, wonderful Magnus, with a fury on his face that told her what he would do next. He drove his blade into the fool's belly. Magnus moved him out of the way and cleaned his sword off before he crouched down over Ashlyn.

"Ash, are you all right?"

She nodded, for the gag was still in her mouth. Magnus pulled it out, and when she held her hands out to him, he untied her, all the time saying, "I'm sorry, I'm sorry but I have to touch you." He was so careful that it brought tears to her eyes. Once he finished untying her, he helped her to a sitting position. Then he held his arms out in front of him, clearly unsure of himself. "I know. You do not like to be touched, but I had no choice, 'twas the only way to untie you. My apologies, lass."

She did the last thing either of them probably expected. She threw herself into those big arms again, wrapping her arms around his neck and sobbing into his shoulder, just as she'd done at the ravine. "My thanks for coming for me. They were to take me…" her breath hitched, "…to Chief Dubh to be his wench."

"Hush. It can wait. Did he hurt you in any way?"

He held her close, and she didn't want to let go, taking in his scent, his warmth, his protectiveness. "Nay."

"Then we need to get out of here." He tugged her behind him

and led the way into the corridor of what appeared to be a small manor home. "I have no idea where Tormod is," Magnus whispered to her. "I saw him go down, but he was not in the chamber with me below stairs."

"I heard them speak of only one prisoner," Ashlyn said, frowning. They glanced into each of the chambers they passed, but Tormod was nowhere to be found.

Ashlyn reached out and took Magnus's hand. "Since we have not seen him, we should leave and search the area to see if he is lying hurt somewhere." Though she had intended to release his hand, she found she did not wish to let go.

Magnus led her out the back door of the building, and they headed back to the center of the burgh, both of them watching for any observers or enemies. As they made their way toward the inns, Magnus stopped in his tracks to survey his surroundings. "Did you hear that? It almost sounded as if someone had called my name."

"Nay. Magnus, how long was I out?" she asked, looking up at the dark sky. "He knocked me over the head. What time is it?"

Magnus tugged her close to him, not willing to let go of her hand, and she found she was quite fine with that. "I do not know. They hit me over the head, also." They did not see anyone they knew. "I'm sure we are too late to meet the others at the inn in the center. But it cannot be too late. The crowd has thinned, but there are still many around."

Someone bellowed his name loud enough for them to both hear, and they jerked around in time to see Jamie, Braden, and Tormod headed their way.

Jamie reached them first. "What happened? Tormod said he was hit over the head."

"The same happened to us," Magnus replied, "but Ashlyn and I were kept in separate chambers inside a manor home not far from here."

Braden snorted. "Any survivors?"

Magnus's trademark grin returned to his face. "Nay. Or mayhap I just knocked the younger one out. The leader did not survive." He glanced at Tormod, who looked a little peaked. "You are hale?"

"I'll be fine. The head aches a wee bit, but it could be worse. I had no idea where you two disappeared to when I came around an hour or so later."

"We learned naught," Jamie said. "Were the lads who took you working for MacNiven?"

"Aye, they plan to be his guards. They called him Chief Dubh, so it must be MacNiven. They were going to meet him at the crossroads on the morrow, hoping to get hired." Ashlyn said, "but I do not think we should discuss it here." She glanced over her shoulder, afraid there might be other lads looking to steal young lasses. Braden and Tormod both looked shocked, but they said naught.

"I agree," Jamie said. "We are late for our meeting with Uncle Logan, and if we arrive too late, he will send more after us. We should return to the royal keep."

They trekked back to the royal castle and met the others inside the gates. Uncle Logan hurried over to them. His voice low and insistent, he called out, "Where the devil have you been? I was about to send a search party out for you."

"Half our team ran into some trouble, but all will be fine by the morrow."

Aunt Gwyneth perused the group, stopping when she reached Ashlyn's. "Not so sure about that. Judging by the number of bruises I see, I think there will be a few headaches by morn. My beautiful niece still has a bit of a black eye from a fist, and now she sports a bump on her head. Logan, let's return to our private chambers and get some refreshments for the three who need it." She wrapped her arm around Ashlyn and hugged her tight.

Once they were inside with some refreshments, Logan closed the door and said, "I hope you have information, because we learned naught."

All eyes turned to Jamie, but he nodded toward Ashlyn. "The only one who learned much is Ashlyn, though Tormod heard something similar. Go ahead. Tell us all."

"Two men hit me over the head and tied me up," Ashlyn began. "When I awakened, the two discussed their plan. According to them, Chief Dubh, whom they described as a man known for wearing a helm or a mask, will be hiring many guards for plenty of coin. They plan to meet him at some crossroads on the morrow, or if not him, some representative of his. They have no idea what his true identity is, nor do they know his purpose."

"And you? Why did they take you?"

"They think that offering him a wench will give them a better chance at getting hired as his guards."

Magnus coughed, a catch in his throat. "A wench? They called you a wench?" She could see his hands fisted at his sides, flexing as he spoke.

"I suspect they'll not be saying it again, will they, Magnus?" Uncle Logan smirked as he glanced from Magnus to Aunt Gwyneth.

Magnus paced in a circle. "Nay."

Logan grinned. "Gwynie, you look as though you are still twenty and four. We could plant you as a wench, see where they take you."

"Logan, you have too many ideas," his wife said, rolling her eyes. "I think we all need rest. We did not get much sleep last night. Can we not go to our rooms? There's naught more to do this eve." She settled her hand on Ashlyn's shoulder, and the touch gave her a sense of comfort. That was happening more and more these days, she realized.

Ashlyn missed her mother and Gracie, and even her stepsire and her brothers. Mayhap Gracie had been right about regretting this journey. Why had she insisted on coming here? Her head pounded more than she wished to admit. She reached up to hold the side of her head to stop the vibrations that seemed to go through her. Uncle Logan glanced at her and his gaze narrowed, so she dropped her hand, not wanting to upset him.

"Another thing I overheard near the inn was that a storm is brewing. We will not get snowed in here, will we, Uncle Logan?" Ashlyn couldn't bear the thought of being stuck here. How many times had she been attacked? Her head hurt so badly that she could not even think.

Uncle Logan nodded to his wife. "I think rest is a great idea, Gwynie. We can plan our next move in the morn. Well done, Ashlyn. Without your information, we would be hapless. You kept your wits while in a dangerous situation. That is commendable."

As soon as they made it inside their chamber, Ashlyn said, "Aunt Gwyneth, have you any of Aunt Brenna's potions? I do not feel well." She sat on a stool and leaned her head into her hands. The pain was excruciating now, and she knew not what to do. Her cousins and aunt stood around her, as if waiting for her to tell them how to help.

"Come, I do have a powder that I can mix for you," Aunt Gwyneth said, "and I have a water skin here. Let me help you get undressed and into bed. You need a good night's rest, and my guess is you need to keep your head still." She gingerly felt through Ashlyn's hair. The pain spiraled through her head when her aunt found the bump. "Och, you have quite a big bump in the middle of your head. He hit you hard. Sorcha, get me my satchel, please. Once I get Ashlyn settled, I'll see to Magnus and Tormod."

Ashlyn could only follow instructions. She was incapable of speaking or thinking. When she was out of her gown, she fell into the bed on one side and slipped under the covers. She only sat up to drink the concoction her aunt had made for her. As soon as her head settled on the pillow the second time, she fell fast asleep. This time she dreamed about Gracie.

Unfortunately, that dream was followed by a very different one. Her captor touched her again, his hands running over her hips, her breasts, and she couldn't fight him this time, no matter what she tried. She attempted to kick him, but he only laughed and laughed and groped her more. But then his face changed to resemble the man at the beach, and then the one man became two.

A bang from somewhere awoke her, and she found herself staring into Magnus's eyes. Aunt Gwyneth's hand was on her shoulder shaking her.

"What is it?" Magnus asked, his face drawn.

As soon as she regained her bearings, she whispered, "My apologies, 'twas naught. Just a bad dream. I was back…"

Magnus let out a deep sigh as he ran a hand over his face and through his hair. Aunt Gwyneth gave him a light push, and only then did Ashlyn notice that her cousins had roused and were staring at her with wide eyes. "Go, Magnus," Aunt Gwyneth said. "I'll take care of her. I'm sure she was having nightmares about the man who abducted her."

Magnus gazed into Ashlyn's eyes. "You're sure you want me to leave?"

She nodded, not wishing to disturb him any longer, though she wished for naught more than to be wrapped in his protective arms again.

Magnus left the chamber, and Ashlyn's cousins instantly fell back against their pillows. Everyone was clearly as exhausted as she was. "Forgive me, Auntie."

"Here, come over onto this big chair and sit with me," her aunt said, pointing into the corner of the chamber. "My guess is you have not really told anyone all that happened to you tonight, and you must. You'll feel better if you tell me about it."

Ashlyn knew she wouldn't fall back asleep, so she moved out of bed and did as her aunt had suggested. The two managed to squeeze into the huge chair together, and when Aunt Gwyneth wrapped her arms around her, she leaned her head onto her shoulder. She loved all her aunts and uncles. How wonderful they were, each special in his or her own way.

"He touched you, did he not?" Aunt Gwyneth whispered.

The sounds from the bed made her believe her cousins had fallen back asleep, so she decided to tell her aunt the truth. "Aye. He groped me when my hands were tied up. I could not stop him, but then I recalled something Robbie had told me, so I shoved my knee hard between his legs and he yelled, saying he would kill me."

"Well done. You hurt him where it pains a man most."

"Aunt Gwyneth, may I ask you a personal question?"

"Sure. I'll answer if I can."

"You were almost sold as a wench, 'tis true?"

"Aye, 'tis true."

"Then how could you allow another man to touch you? Every time a man touches me, I have bad memories, and I hate it. Yet I adored my two brothers when they were just bairns. I would love to have a family someday, but I fear I could never bear a man's touch again. But my mother did, and she's so happy." It was something she'd never told anyone before. Though Ashlyn pretended she never wished to marry, her heart longed for it, longed for a husband and bairns to love. She simply thought she *couldn't* marry.

"Your stepsire is a special man, 'tis why she's happy. That's my answer to you. Women are often abused, 'tis sad to say, but lads are stronger than lasses, and some lads take advantage. Not all lads are bad, though you've met many that are. Believe me that when you find the right one, you will enjoy his touch."

"Do you…" she swallowed before she asked the most difficult

question. "Do you enjoy Uncle Logan's touch, or do you only bear it because you love him? Sometimes, I do not mind Magnus's touch, but only when I am frightened."

"Aye, I enjoy my husband's touch. When two people love each other, 'tis verra special for them to give each other pleasure. Your uncle is the only lad for me, but it does not bother me to hug other clanmates I trust."

Ashlyn absorbed this for a moment. No one else seemed to react to a man's touch with fear the way she did. "There must be something wrong with me."

"Mayhap you have not found the right man yet. I do not know what happened to you when you were younger, but we all know you were old enough to understand the abuse your mother suffered after your sire's death. She is a strong lass, and did all she could for you and Gracie. Your aunt Maddie was hurt by lads, too, and she will tell you that it was a verra long time before she could tolerate Uncle Alex's touch."

"Aye, Aline told me that." Ashlyn shook her head. "I could not believe how quickly she married Jake."

"Every one of us is different. Aline fell in love with Jake, and they may have difficulties in the bed chamber they do not tell you about. Some women hold in their suffering, and mayhap that is Aline's way, but it usually comes out somehow. I did not like a man's touch either, and my emotions affected the way I handled my bow and arrow." She paused. "But you are adjusting to Magnus's touch? 'Tis a good sign. It tells me you trust Magnus."

"Sometimes it frightens me, and sometimes it feels good when he holds me. He held me when he found me last eve, and it was verra comforting. But I know Magnus would never hurt me."

"That is the largest part of it, Ashlyn. You have to trust the man, and when you do, 'twill happen."

Could she dare to dream?

# CHAPTER TEN

Magnus climbed off the floor in the morn as soon as he heard footsteps in the passageway. His hand immediately went to his head. Hellfire, they'd hit him pretty hard the night before. His next thought was for Ashlyn. Was she suffering the way he was?

Logan emerged from his chamber and came to a stop in front of him. "Any problems last night?"

Magnus brushed the sleep out of his eyes. "Aye, Ashlyn had nightmares, but Gwyneth handled it. I noticed she has a bigger bump than I do. My head is paining me still, so I fear hers must be even worse."

Logan rubbed his own head as if in sympathy. "I'm thinking of sending you and Ashlyn home," he said after a moment. "Now that we know what MacNiven is doing, we can focus our efforts. He's not in the caves of the Highlands as I'd feared, and he is not selling slaves. 'Twill be easier to find him if he is indeed searching to hire guards. Braden, Jamie, and the other guards are willing to stay and help, but if she is in that much pain, mayhap you should take her home. 'Tis not the first time she has been ill treated. I'm not sure she can handle more."

"I doubt she will choose to leave. She wanted to be a guard."

"I think Ashlyn may choose to go home. She was not expecting to be hurt or kidnapped. And my other concern is the weather. I checked and found out there is a storm brewing. You are aware that you could get snowed out of returning to the Highlands for a time. You are all certainly welcome to stay with Clan Ramsay until spring, but I do not think Ashlyn would handle being away from her family that long. 'Twould be a long time for her to spend away from her loved ones."

"You may suggest it, but I do not expect her to accept it." Hadn't Ashlyn always wanted to travel with the guards? Now that she'd gotten them this much closer to MacNiven, there was no chance she'd back down.

"And if she does agree to make the journey home, I expect you to act with the honor of a Grant guard."

Magnus chuckled a little at that. "She would stab me while I slept if I tried to touch her."

"Think on it. I head below stairs to arrange for a chamber and food to break our fast. We shall see how she fares today." Logan patted his shoulder and headed toward the stairs.

A short time later, the door to the women's chamber opened and Gwyneth popped out. "Was that my husband's voice I just heard?"

"Aye, he went below stairs to arrange for a place for us to break our fast."

"Good, I shall return promptly, Magnus. You're on guard here. The lasses are almost ready."

He smiled and nodded. The door opened again a few moments later, and Ashlyn stepped out. "Good morn to you, Magnus." The dark circles under her eyes worried him.

"And to you. How do you fare? Does your head pain you the way mine does?"

"Aye."

Then she said one of the last things he'd expected to hear.

"I wish to go home," Ashlyn declared.

He was stunned. "You do? Do you not think the pain in your head would ease more quickly if you stayed here and rested? The cold can be ruthless."

"Nay. I miss my mother and everyone else." There was a hitch in her voice as she said it. "My head is in so much pain I do not think I could help Uncle Logan at all. Though we have not discovered the location of Cedrica or Lorna, it does not appear that he is selling women, or that he is doing aught than he's done before. He's hiring guards to fight someone, and I helped to uncover his plans. We may never find the women. I have achieved as much as I'd hoped to."

"That surprises me, but I am willing to go along with you."

"You are? I thought mayhap Jamie and Braden would go with me and you would stay here."

"Jamie is in charge of the mission, on order of his laird. He cannot leave. Braden is having the time of his life. He will not be pleased if he's sent home with you. I'm an old man who is content with the slow life at times, so I'd be happy to escort you home. I was also ordered to be your protector on this trip." It was true. He wasn't familiar enough with the Ramsays to be comfortable there. He'd rather go home. True, his Rhona was gone, but it was still his home with Mada and Sim and all his friends.

"I'm a wee bit embarrassed, but I will admit to what I told my auntie this morn."

"What could you be embarrassed about?"

"That I could not bear it if we were snowed out of the Highlands. I'd prefer to be snowed in. I was surprised by how difficult the journey was, and we may not be able to make it if we wait another sennight or two. I do not wish to be separated from my family until spring."

"Talk to your uncle Logan when we go below stairs. As I said, I am willing."

Before Magnus could even process the change of events, he and Ashlyn were saying their goodbyes. They left after packing their things and stocking their saddlebags with blocks of cheese, ale, and oatcakes. Ashlyn wished to ride her own horse, though Logan had tried to convince her that she should ride with Magnus. It was unconventional for a lass and a lad to travel alone together, but Ashlyn was older, and everyone knew her opinion of men.

He was glad she had refused to ride with him. It would have driven him mad to ride all the way to Grant land with her sweet bottom nestled up against his cock. It probably would have broken off in the cold. Distance. He needed distance from her soft curves. Even when he helped her mount, he had to turn his head away. One glance and he was hard.

*A few days*, he told himself, *that's how long your torture will last.*

The first day of their journey was uneventful. They chatted comfortably, and found a nice empty cave to sleep in. The second day changed everything. Just after the sun was highest, Ashlyn lifted her head up to the winds and tugged her mantle tight around her. They had just traveled through a narrow ravine, the kind that would be impassable during snow storms. It was one checkpoint he was pleased they had put behind them.

"Magnus, the winds are changing." Her head tipped back, then turned to pick up the direction of the breeze. She had to yell for him to hear her.

"Aye, they are. The temperature is dropping, too. I do not like this. 'Twas a wise move wearing trews under your skirts."

"And woolen socks under my trews."

"Ashlyn, I think there is a storm brewing. We've made it through one of the toughest ravines, aye, but I'd suggest we search for shelter. I don't want to be caught in the middle of a heavy snowstorm. I'd prefer to tuck into a cave or a cottage and wait it out, see if we can't find cover for the horses, as well. The winds keep building and once the snow starts coming down, 'twill be hard to see. 'Tis how people get lost in the Highlands. I do not wish to be one of them, especially since I have not made this journey as often as your cousins."

"Do you have any idea where to go?"

"Mayhap someone will take us in."

"I hope it does not drop enough snow to prevent our passage after the storm," Ashlyn said, biting her lip. They stared up at the changing skies—shades of grays and blues flickered past. Occasional beams of the sun broke through, but the cloud cover was already thick. A few snowflakes floated through the air, a tease of what was to come. "Magnus, I am freezing already and night is just beginning to fall. The temperature is still dropping. Do you know of a cave nearby?"

"Nay, but I do recall seeing a deserted hut when we came south. It was not far from the ravine, just off the path a bit. I noticed it when I moved into the bushes to relieve myself when we stopped."

The farther they went, the heavier the snowfall became. They traveled for a bit before something caught Magnus's eye. He pointed off the path. "There. I can just see the edge of the roof. I'll lead the way. Follow me." They'd almost made it when Magnus held his hand up, indicating the need to stop.

"What is it?" she asked. "It looks deserted to me. And there's a lean-to for the horses, a well-made one with walls on three sides. This seems perfect."

"Aye." He pointed off the trail. "I'll take that downed tree before it's buried in snow. My horse will be able to pull it out. I have an axe, but 'tis a small one. I won't be able to drop any big trees. We'll need the wood to keep warm."

She nodded, moving ahead of him so he could tie the tree to his horse. "Do you need help?"

"Nay. I have it." He gave her his usual big smile as he climbed back onto his horse. "Our luck. 'Tis a mighty log. We can dry it in the lean-to and the snow is deep enough for it to slide easily."

They stopped in front of the hut and Magnus climbed down. "I'll make sure 'tis empty before we settle the horses."

"And get rid of any critters who've made it their home, will you not?"

He couldn't help but laugh when she cringed—he'd seen her shoot a man with an arrow, after all. Most critters were already deep in hibernation. He moved inside the hut, surprised to see it was in decent condition other than a few cobwebs he knocked out of the way. After yelling the all clear to Ashlyn, he continued his examination. The hearth was still in good shape, and there were several pieces of dry wood stacked next to it and a pot hanging above it. One pallet sat to the side and a table and three stools were arranged next to the opposite wall. A few utensils decorated the mostly empty shelves. Aye, it would do just fine.

He stepped back outside into the bitter wind, and stared at Ashlyn on her horse. She pointed off to the side, a smug smile on her face. "'Twas my turn for dinner. I killed it, so you can retrieve it."

He turned his head and almost jumped for joy. "A pheasant? You shot a pheasant in this weather?" He ran over to pick it up. "Nice, Ash. He's got lots of meat on him. I'll give you a kiss for this one."

A scowl crossed her face. "Like hell. No kisses. Keep your hands away."

"But 'twould be my lips, not my hands." He winked at her as he led the horses over to the lean-to behind the cottage.

"No lips, no hands."

"May I use my hands to help you down? You have enough material covering you so as not to feel my touch."

"I'll accept that, but only because 'tis hard to move with trews and a skirt."

They settled the horses, grabbed their belongings, and moved inside. Ashlyn walked around, taking in her surroundings. "Aye, this will do," she finally said. "Well done, Magnus."

"You settle yourself, and I'll go feed the horses the oats we brought. Then I'll cut the wood, bring some inside, and set the rest to drying. This snow is coming down fast and hard now. If you have needs to take care of, I'd do it now off in the woods before the snow gets any deeper. By morn, we'll both be going right outside the door."

She gave him a fierce scowl that made him laugh, then made her way toward the door. Ashlyn's innocence made her an easy target for goading. He'd already learned multiple ways to tease her. He whistled as he held the door for her.

She set her satchel down and grabbed some ladles and bowls from the shelf. "I'll clean some things and gather enough snow so we can keep a broth cooking. I've got turnips and carrots to use in it."

"What? Why the hell do you have turnips and carrots?"

She moved over to the hearth to grab the pot. "I always carry turnips and carrots."

Ashlyn was like no other lass he'd ever met. He looked forward to finding out more about her, but now was not the time. "All the better for us. Pheasant, cheese, and vegetables. We'll survive. Snow for water. Do what you must, lass. If you need me, come and get me. I'll be behind the lean-to with the horses."

Ashlyn woke up shivering in the middle of the night. Even with the extra plaid Magnus had given her, she could not get warm. She rolled onto her other side and checked the floor to make sure Magnus was still there. The wind howled outside, and she imagined the snow still swirling through the dark sky. She'd never be able to rest in this cold, dark place. How she missed her sister, her favorite person in the world to huddle next to in the cold when the temperature dropped, though Robbie and his brothers had built a much sturdier cottage than this one. She could hear the wind whistling through some of the holes between the stones. Their home offered much more protection, and Robbie had several deer pelts hanging inside the stone walls as a further deterrent to the cold, along with many pelts for the cushioned bed, so much more comfortable than the thin pallet beneath her.

"Lass, your teeth are chattering." Magnus's voice carried from the cold stone floor.

"I know," she whispered. "My apologies for waking you, Magnus."

"There is a solution."

"There is? Och, nay, it would require touching, would it not?"

"Aye, it would, but I vow on my honor that I will give you my warmth only. I will not touch you inappropriately. All you need to do is lean back against me, you need not face me."

She shivered again as another blast of wind hit the stone walls of the small hut. Mayhap she should take him at his word. She'd leaned against him at the Buchans' keep and he had not done anything inappropriate, and he had been mighty warm.

"Promise not to touch me except to my back? I'd just like to lean against you as I did in the Buchan's solar. I'm so cold, Magnus. I cannot stop my trembling."

Magnus stood up from his spot on the floor, dragging his plaid along with him. "I promise. If you do not, you may never wake again, and I do not think your mother would be too happy with me."

"All right. I'll turn on my side first." She rolled over so her front faced the wall, and she shivered again just from the small movement. The pallet moved as soon as Magnus put his weight on it, and the shifting of the mattress rolled her against him. "What are you doing?"

"Patience. I am a large man if you have not noticed, lass. It takes a moment to adjust, and I'll only touch you once."

She did as he asked for one reason only...she could already feel his heat. He arranged himself behind her, turning her so her back was to his chest and his back was to the cold stone wall. She couldn't help it, she moaned from the sheer heat of him.

"Lass, you're like an icicle. How the hell are you still breathing? You'll have me shivering with you. Allow me to put my arms around you just for a wee bit to heat you through." He tucked the plaid around her legs.

She nodded. His arms came around her and she wished to melt into him. Hellfire, had she ever felt aught as good as this? As soon as his huge arms covered her, she closed her eyes with a sigh. She fell asleep in seconds from sheer exhaustion.

Later in the night, she heard a sound. The bastard Norseman. She could feel his hands on her, the hands that had awoken her. Flailing, she tried to wake Magnus to stop the cruel man, but he slept on. The fool tried to touch her everywhere, so she hit him. Then he moved on to Gracie. His hands were all over her sister, her dear sister, and she was supposed to be protecting her. Her sweet sister Gracie counted on her. She swung and swung to get him away from her until she screamed.

She screamed and screamed and screamed.

The next thing she knew, Magnus was shaking her. "Ashlyn, wake up. You're having a nightmare. 'Tis a bad dream. I'm here, I'll not let him at you again. Wake up."

And finally she did. She woke up and stared at him standing in the middle of the hut, but in that moment he looked like the bastard who had come after her and Gracie. So she swung and swung. At first he held her hands to stop her from connecting with his flesh, but then he let her go.

"Leave me be. Do not touch me," she shrieked. Tears stung her eyes as she fought to get away from him. His smell, his dirty hands. The bastard who had come for them near the rocks.

"Go ahead, lass. Let it out. Keep swinging if 'twill make you feel better."

"And do not touch my sister either. Keep your hands away. You're dirty, you're disgusting."

She connected with him over and over, but he never stepped back, never stopped her.

"Who? Who is it you're hitting?" he whispered.

"The man. The disgusting man who came along after my mother was attacked. He woke me up. Gracie and I were hiding behind the rocks, then we slept over by the trees and he found us." Her hands continued to windmill, but without much force.

"What did he do?"

"He touched me. His hands were between my legs when I woke up, and I hit him and hit him. And then he hit me."

She screamed in frustration and rage, swinging at Magnus again. Why was she swinging at him?

"What happened next? Did he leave you be?"

"Aye. He did. He left me and he went for Gracie. When I

followed him, he had his hands on Gracie's private parts. He was touching her, and I swung at him and he screamed and I screamed and Gracie cried."

"What else?"

"Why? Why are you doing this?" Her tears flooded in twin rivers down her cheeks. She cried as she continued to hit Magnus. She knew she wasn't hurting him—she didn't *want* to hurt him, but she still swung at him. The fury was inside her again, and it needed to get out.

"Why am I doing what?"

"Why do you allow me to hit you? Why? I should not do it, yet I cannot stop. Stop me, please."

# CHAPTER ELEVEN

Magnus just stared at her in shock. Something huge had hit him, and it wasn't a wee fist from a broken woman—it was a piece of her soul. He'd sworn this would never happen again, and yet it had.

She finally fell against his chest, sobbing, and he wrapped his arms around her. "Why, Magnus? Stop me, please stop me. Why do you not stop me?"

"Because…"

"Because why?"

He held her as she continued to sob, the pain she must have endured all these years finally coming out. He might as well just say it. "Because I love you." Magnus could feel her entire body tense in his arms, and her sobbing stopped. What kind of fool was he to have said such words? He'd sworn never to use them again. And yet he had no desire to deny them or take them back.

She pulled back, gazing into his eyes. "What did you say?" The confusion in her face told him all he needed to know. His feelings weren't reciprocated. It hadn't even occurred to her to consider him that way.

"I said I love you. There. I've said what's in my heart. I no longer wish to deny it. I love you, Ashlyn, and I wish to help you fight your demons. And if hitting me helps you fight them, then I will allow it."

She just stared at him, and he had no idea what to do next. Would she hate him for feeling as he did?

"Why? Why do you love me? I'm not like Rhona at all." She swiped at the tears on her face.

He tugged her back over to the pallet and sat down with her on his lap, cocooning her in his warmth. She was still a block of ice, even after expending all that energy swinging.

"I know you're not like Rhona, but I love you for who you are. You are a verra strong, proud, beautiful woman. I understand you may not feel the same way about me, but if you give us a chance, you may someday. I can wait. I have naught at home except my two dogs."

She leaned against him. "I have always wanted a family," she said in a whisper, "but I know a lass cannot carry if she will not let her husband touch her. I…I do not know if I could do that. I know how it happens, and all I ever think of is that awful man and the awful Norseman who beat my mother. I'll disappoint you for sure, Magnus."

"But you have not minded my touch. You have allowed it when I thought you would react negatively. Mayhap you are changing. I can be a patient man, Ashlyn. I would like to help you get past this atrocity that burdens you."

"What you say is true. I have not minded your touch the way I have in the past. I…I trust you, I guess 'tis what it is."

"I'll accept that to start. Was there another man before that? Before the Norse came?"

"Nay, my mother was protective of us."

"Tell me all that happened that night, after Robbie took your mother away."

She sighed, but then began her story—a story she had never told anyone. "I did not think Mama was coming back. When I felt it was safe, we walked around to find a neighbor, anyone, but they were all gone. The cottages had been burned, so there was naught inside. We had heard the Norse were coming, so my mother had packed some food for us in a satchel in case we needed to run. We had food and water, but Gracie was verra young, so I had to take care of her." She sniffled and wiped her tears again.

"You feel bad about what happened to Gracie, worse than you do about what happened to you."

"Aye, I was supposed to protect her."

"It sounds as if you did protect her. Continue with your story."

"I returned to the spot my mother had found for us to hide in because there was a small group of trees nearby. We fell asleep and I did not wake up until I felt his hands on me. I fought him, and he was furious, so he hit me and knocked me out. The next time I woke up, he was touching Gracie and I jumped up to attack him."

"Did you know him?"

"Nay."

"What happened next?"

"I hit him and hit him and he ran away."

"So you did protect her." He ran his hand up and down her forearm, trying to warm her.

"I guess I did, but…"

"But what?" Magnus knew there was more, but she was not ready to tell all yet.

"Naught. 'Tis all I remember."

One step at a time. "Ashlyn, I promise you I will never touch you unless you want me to, and I also promise that the moment you say nay, I'll walk away."

"What if you kiss me one day, and I ask you to stop?"

"I will."

"But some say a man cannot stop when he is past a certain point."

"Whoever told you that is lying. A man can always stop. We may not want to, but we can."

"Then mayhap I could try sometime with you." She placed her hand in his and he squeezed it, a light feathery touch.

"I know why you carry the carrots and turnips." He kissed her hair, then nuzzled her neck just a touch to see if she would accept him, and he was pleased that she did.

"Why?"

"Because you want to make sure you'll never go hungry again."

A single tear slid down her left cheek and she smiled. "Aye, 'tis true."

"Did you go hungry often?"

"Aye, before we came to Clan Grant. I gave most of my food to Gracie once she was old enough. I was used to being hungry. She was not."

"You are generous and loyal. I'll add those two qualities to my reasons."

"Reasons for what?" She gazed up at him.

"Reasons for loving you."

They gazed into each other's eyes and then she licked her lips, and he could feel her pulse increase.

"Will you promise to stop kissing me if I say nay?"

"Aye. I already made you that promise, and it holds forever." He brushed a stray tear from her cheek.

She giggled. "Forever?"

"Aye, until the day I die, I promise to stop when you ask me to."

"Then kiss me."

"Lass, it seems only right for me to say something before we become more involved. After my Rhona, that is…I do not…I do not know if I could ever be a good husband again. If we do this, I want your commitment as an adult woman, not a young lass with her head in the clouds. If we do this, we should marry. Just know that it will be difficult for me. It does not change that I love you, but my heart is torn between two."

"I understand what you ask. 'Struth is I have always been curious, but I do not know if I could be a good wife either. My mother taught me that I marry the man I give myself to, but I am so confused right now. And I cannot say that I love you. I have strong feelings for you, and I do trust you, but is that enough for you? I cannot promise what will happen on this night or how far I can go, but I am interested in learning more about what it feels to be in a man's arms."

"Are you interested in marriage? I must know this first. Would you be willing if you carry our bairn?"

"Aye. I have always wished to marry and have bairns, but I know not if 'tis possible. I promised myself I would not marry if I could not tolerate a man's touch. I have yet to learn the truth of that. If I cannot, then we need not have this discussion. Is this acceptable to you?"

Magnus didn't need any more encouragement. He'd been staring at those luscious lips of hers for some time now. He kissed her, a tender kiss designed not to frighten her, but to let her know how much he did care, how much he wanted her. He moved his mouth over hers, urging her to part her lips so he could really taste her. To his surprise, he heard a soft mewling sound in the back of her throat that motivated him more than words could ever do.

She parted her lips and he swept his tongue inside her mouth, but slowly, allowing her to get used to him. He teased her, hoping she would meet him, and she finally did, her sweet tongue touching his for a brief moment before she jumped up and said, "Nay."

"Nay it is." He ran his hand down his face to calm his needs, but it had gone better than he had expected. He had worried she would push him away at the touch of his tongue, but she had not.

Because she was a bold woman, something he'd known all along. He'd also wager she'd be an equal partner in bed, if he could ever get her that far. Once she discovered her sensuality, she would probably be insatiable.

How would he get her to that point?

She rubbed her hands down her arms. "Are you angry with me?"

"Nay. I promise I will not get angry with you if you tell me nay."

He stood from the pallet and sat on the stool, resting his elbows on his knees, clasping his hands together. "I promise, Ashlyn. Now answer me this. Did I hurt you?"

"Nay." She stared up at the ceiling, and even though it was still dark, he could tell she was struggling to keep the tears from falling.

"Come, let's go back and get some sleep." He held his hand out to her.

She placed her hand in his, but she didn't move. "Kiss me again, but while we're standing, so I can back away quickly if I must."

He quirked his brow at her, but she did not change her mind. "All right." He moved toward her, almost touching but not quite. He cupped her face with his hands and touched his forehead to hers. "You're sure?"

"Aye."

He kissed her, molding his lips with hers, parting her lips with just a bit of pressure, and she gave in to him immediately. Angling his mouth over hers, he savored the taste of her, wishing she would give him the chance to pleasure her.

She moaned and leaned in to him, pressing her breasts against him, enough so he could tell her nipples had peaked, even through the rough fabric, though mayhap that was only from the cold.

He pulled back, "Ash, may I feel your soft skin against mine?"

Her answer came out in a breathy pant that pleased him. "Aye."

His hand moved to the ribbons on the front of her shift and he tugged on them, surprised to feel her hand assisting him with his task. When he freed her breast from its confines and cupped the full mound in his hand, he groaned with pleasure, rubbing his thumb across her nipple. She responded to his touch by arching her breast into his hand, her hand gripping his bicep tightly. Aye, she would be a passionate one. Her soft sounds urged him on, so he moved his hand lower, grateful she'd removed her trews before climbing into bed.

His hand moved down toward her hip and over to her belly, and he knew it was wrong the moment he did it.

She jumped back, "Nay."

"All right." He stepped back, his raging arousal speaking to him even though he denied it. Spinning on his heel, he opened the door and stepped outside into the cold blast of winter.

"Magnus?"

"What?" he bellowed. He took a deep sigh as the cold helped douse the fire in his veins.

"You promised."

"Promised? Aye, I did. You said nay, I stopped." He stepped back into the doorway. "I stopped, just as you asked."

"Close the door, please. And you're angry. You said you wouldn't get angry if I said nay." The frown on her face told him everything.

Despite all she'd been through, despite how strong and courageous she was, Ashlyn was in many ways an innocent. He rubbed his hand in his hair on the top of his head. "Ashlyn, I'm not mad. 'Tis just that men…men sometimes…get excited. 'Tis hard to put an end to it that quickly." He stared at her, wondering if she understood any of what he said. Hell but his mind was spinning.

"Excited?"

"Aye."

"About what?"

"About you, lass." He sauntered over to her and leaned over to gaze into her big brown eyes. "You excite me. The feeling of you in my arms, the thought of making love to you, stirs my blood." He leaned over to whisper into her ear. "I want you."

"You do? I do? I…I'm confused."

"We've done enough for one night, and I promise you that you did not anger me. Do you believe that?" He took her hand in his and brought it up to his lips, kissing her knuckle.

"Nay. I want more. I want you to touch me there. Mayhap 'twill erase the other from my mind. Mayhap 'tis what I need, Magnus. Please? I'll try my best not to stop you this time."

"You are sure this is what you want?"

"I am. I...want you, too. And I cannot be sure how I will feel after, but I would like to try." She gazed up at him between her lashes and he was lost. "What if this will put an end to my nightmares? Mayhap a good touch will end my fears. I do not want my nightmares to go on any longer. Please?"

Hell, she'd be the death of him yet. He scooped her up in his arms and placed her on the pallet, as gingerly as he could. "Lass, I'm going to take your shift off, and I'll keep you warm with my heat. I promise."

She nodded and held up her arms for him. He decided to keep his plaid on for her shyness. Since she had brothers, his anatomy was not likely to shock her, but he decided to play it safe. Plaids could come off in a hurry if need be—the true reason a Scotsman wore his plaid, to his mind.

He covered her body with his, and she moaned as soon as he held himself up on his elbows, caressing her soft silky hair, tucking the wild strands away from her face. "You are happy so far?"

"Aye, you are so warm."

"Hot, lass. I am hot for you." He sucked on her lower lip and cupped her breast with his hand, sighing in pleasure at the feel of its fullness. "Ashlyn, you are every bit as beautiful as I knew you would be." He rolled her nipple between his thumb and forefinger and smiled at her reaction to his touch. She was a wonderful mix of delight and confusion. Aye, she had no idea what was coming, but he had all the time in the world to bring her to climax. And that he would.

"Do not be afraid, but I'm going to kiss your breast."

She sighed, putting her hands on his head as he lowered his lips to her nipple, kissing and licking every corner of the taut peak, teasing and tasting until she writhed beneath him. He feared his hardness would frighten her, but he was unable to control it. If she would just spread her legs, he could slip inside. He reached up to his shoulder and tugged off his plaid, tossing it to the side. Her panting urged him forward, so he took her nipple in his mouth, suckling her until she cried out. He moved to the other breast, holding it in his hand, caressing it before he lowered his tongue to her nipple.

Her hips bucked toward him, and he smiled. His hand reached down to the curls at her juncture and touched her there. His arousal rubbed against her thigh and he groaned, wanting so much to plant himself inside her and bury his seed there. But his sire's teachings told him he should not finish unless she agreed to marriage.

"Nay."

Magnus thought he must have heard her wrong. "What?"

"Nay, I said nay!" She screamed in his ear and he bolted off the pallet and onto his feet.

She jumped up behind him, grabbing her shift to cover herself. "I'm sorry, but I cannot…"

Magnus tipped his head back and roared, then opened the door to step outside.

"Magnus, you promised. You said you would not get angry, and you're angry. You're bellowing like a sick animal. And you're going outside to get away from me."

"Arghhhhh! I'm not angry! I'm going outside because I must stick something in the snowbank." He slammed the door behind him.

His cock.

Hellfire, how else could he stop this raging need inside him? He'd stick it right into the snowbank. Mayhap then his mind could function again.

# CHAPTER TWELVE

Slud, now what had she done? Ashlyn stared after him, wondering what was wrong. She donned her shift quickly and then moved toward the door, wishing to follow him, yet afraid. What the hell did he intend to stick in the snowbank? Her eyes widened when it dawned on her what he meant, so she reached for the handle and flung the door open.

He stood directly in front of her, a gleam in his eye.

"You are all right?" she whispered. She knew he must be, he wore that dastardly grin of his again.

"Aye, I am fine."

"You are not angry?"

"Nay, I am not angry." His voice was so soft that it caressed her skin. "I am a man of my word. I will not say 'tis easy, but I am still a man of my word."

"Did you stick it in the snowbank?"

He chuckled. "Nay, the cold air was enough."

"May I see it?"

He maneuvered her back inside and closed the door behind them. "See what?"

"Your cock?"

He choked. "Lass, must you be so blunt?"

"What else should I call it? 'Tis what most lads call it. If you do not wish for me to be afraid of it, I must see it."

"Nay, you may not see it."

His horrified expression told her she would not get what she wanted. "Why? I wish to look at it to see what's coming." She'd changed her brothers' raggies, so she'd seen one before, but Magnus's felt enormous against her thigh.

He moved to stand just a breath away from her, staring into her eyes. "Nay, I do not think 'tis wise for you to study that part of me, at least not in the manner you have in mind. If you are curious about aught, tell me."

"I…I do not think we will fit together." She'd felt it against her leg. There was no way it would fit where it was supposed to. She stared off at the wall.

He laughed, tracing a line down her jaw with his finger. "Lass, let me worry about that. We will fit just fine. 'Tis my job to be sure we do."

She pondered this for a moment, especially since she really wasn't interested in examining his manhood up close. Still, it had looked quite painful. Suddenly, a warm feeling washed through her body, and she realized Magnus's hands were roaming all over her skin, his heat singeing her through the material.

"Close your eyes."

"Why?"

"Because you must learn to trust me. Close your eyes and focus on naught but my touch."

"Why are you allowed to touch me if I cannot touch you?"

"I did not say you could not touch me. I asked you not to *study* me. 'Tis most different. But why not close your eyes and just let yourself feel? Lass, I want to give you pleasure."

She paused before answering, but even though it still unnerved her, she wanted to experience this with him. "All right."

"Then close your eyes, and enjoy my touch."

She nodded, closing her eyes. "I wish to touch you, too."

He reached for her hand and placed it on his male parts. "Aye, feel how it grows as I touch you, and you'll understand how beautiful you are to me."

His cock was quite warm, and her eyes popped open as soon as she felt him grow in her hands.

"You promised. Eyes closed." He lifted her shift and ran his hands up her thighs and over her hips.

His hands warmed her, so she closed her eyes again.

"You do trust me, do you not, Ash?"

"I do, Magnus. I trust you." Her hand ran down the length of him, the velvety soft skin that seemed to heat her core on its own. His hardness did not frighten her, though she was still slightly concerned it would not fit. She cupped his ballocks very carefully, as she knew how sensitive they were. She'd seen it first hand in Edinburgh. Vowing to handle him the same gentle way he handled her, she moved her hand back and forth along his shaft.

"Be verra careful what you start, lass."

"But I like it."

He laughed. "I am glad that you do, but do not torture me. Stop thinking and feel."

She let go of him and focused on his hands, the hands that were now cupping her breasts, his thumbs rubbing across the sensitive tips.

"You like that, do you not?"

"Aye." Shocked at how her voice came out in such a husky tone, she stopped speaking and let herself focus instead on *feeling*.

His hands massaged her breasts, and each movement seemed to send an arrow down to her sex. A strange feeling built inside of her, one that made her wish to spread her legs wider, a thought that appalled her, especially since she was still standing.

"Magnus?"

"Aye?"

"When you come inside me, 'twill hurt, will it not?"

"Aye, for a maiden it hurts the first time, but being a maiden is not important to me. Whether you are a maiden or not, the pain shall pass and will be replaced with a yearning."

"A yearning for what?"

He sighed, leaning down to nuzzle her neck. "For completion." His hands moved from her breasts back to her hips, then down to her bottom. He ran his fingers over the round globes of her backside with the lightest of touches, causing her to squirm and arch toward him.

"Hold still and let me do that again."

"The same place? But why?"

"Aye, just allow me to caress your skin there, see if you like it."

"Aye," she said, her voice small. When he touched her again, she was shocked to feel the hitching in her breath, the unsettling in her belly, and the yearning for more. "Magnus?"

"Do you like my hands there, teasing you, stroking your soft skin?"

She opened her mouth to speak, but a moan came out instead.

Vaguely, she heard him chuckle just before his mouth claimed hers again, but this time it was different. This kiss was rough, demanding. His lips moved over hers, and his tongue invaded her senses. She touched her tongue to his, and the growl he pushed out told her that he had liked it. His tongue explored her mouth, pushing deeper, and she found herself gripping his arms, her nails digging into his hard muscles.

"I'm going to touch you there now, and you'll understand why you'll fit." His hand moved over to the vee of her curls, parting her slowly and teasing her entrance. "Do you feel how wet you are for me? You are ready for me. Do you wish to do this?"

"Aye." Her voice came out in a whisper, but she did not care, she would do anything with this man right now.

He lifted her into his arms and settled her on the pallet, then moved to the side of her so he could take her nipple in his mouth again. His hand found her entrance again and he inserted his finger, moving it in and out in a most torturous rhythm.

"Magnus. It feels so good."

He pulled back and smiled at her, that smile she loved. "Aye, because you are hot and slick and wet for me. Your juices cover my hand. If you wish it, we shall finish. 'Tis your choice, love."

"Aye. Do it, please." Her legs spread wide on their own volition and he moved above her, settling between her legs. Reaching down for his cock, he teased her entrance even more, and she could not stand the torture any longer. "Please, Magnus."

He gripped her hips and plunged inside of her with one move. She squirmed underneath him, shocked at the pain of his invasion. A tear leaked out and trailed down her cheek.

"Shhhh, wee one. Trust me. 'Twill be better in a moment. You shall adjust to me."

He continued to whisper sweet words in her ear, so she gripped him, her hands laced around his neck and her face buried in his shoulder as she waited for the pain to subside. A few moments later, she moved, pleased to see he was right. "Are we done now? Can you take it out?"

"Nay, we are not done. I will not leave you until you are satisfied."

"I am satisfied."

"Give me two minutes and see if you still say those same

words." After kissing her forehead and then her lips, he began to move inside of her again, sliding out and thrusting slowly, each time becoming easier. Something started to *build* inside her, though she knew not what.

She could hear him panting, and was surprised to hear her own breathing matched his. "You are right. I am not satisfied yet. Keep going."

Magnus gripped her hips again and rode her, hitting a spot that started a fire inside of her. Then he did something she had not expected at all. He reached between them and touched her between the legs, right above where they were connected, massaging her and caressing her until she screamed, careening over an edge she hadn't seen coming. He continued his assault on her until she heard him groan, his hands holding her hips, clutching her the same way she had clutched him, as if they never wished to be apart again.

Suddenly, the world took on new meaning.

Magnus had trouble coming up with the right words. Had it been that long since he'd held a woman he loved in his arms, felt her shudder with the essence of her climax?

He had only one thing he wished to say, but he did not think Ashlyn would accept it yet. His primitive instinct shouted inside of him: *Mine, you're mine now, lass.* He wished to tell her how much he loved her, to propose to her, to talk of marriage, but he knew the feeling of love was not reciprocated, so he held his tongue. He could not, so he kept his words to himself, though his heart told him differently. She needed time to adjust to all that had happened between them.

He cradled her in his arms, giving her his heat in the cold of the night. Kissing her forehead, he settled her head on his shoulder, his hand caressing her arm. Neither of them spoke for a few moments, each absorbed with their own thoughts. Finally he said, "Did I please you, Ash?"

"Aye, more than you know," she whispered, kissing his cheek. "And did I please you?"

He laughed and repeated her words. "More than you know... Do you have any regrets?"

"Nay." She cuddled in closer to him. "We should probably sleep, but I fear I cannot yet."

"Why not? Something bothering you?"

"Aye."

He could tell she was having trouble working over whatever was on her mind, so he waited for her to speak. Patience. He just needed patience.

She sighed. "I have more to tell you. But I wish to gather my thoughts for a moment. Promise not to fall asleep?"

"Aye." Was she ready to tell him the rest of her story about the past? How he hoped she would. Part of him feared she'd lost her maidenhead to some brute, but she had not. It had been intact. He climbed off the pallet, deciding he would give her a moment to herself, and found a cloth to wash her. After their repast, they'd filled one of the bowls with snow so it would melt. He pulled a cloth from his sporran and dipped it into the water before returning to her side, sitting on the edge of the pallet.

He blew the warm air of his breath onto the cold cloth.

"What are you doing?" She gave him a strange look telling him she hadn't thought of the blood that was probably on her leg.

"I'm cleaning the blood from your maidenhead." He moved his hand between her thighs, gently moving them apart.

"What?" She stared at her legs. "Oh." She blushed.

"Do not be embarrassed." As he washed the blood from her, she gazed into his eyes, apparently surprised he would so such a thing. "You gave me a wonderful gift," he added.

"Magnus, I stabbed him."

His hand froze, and he had to force himself to continue. Was she referring to the man that had been touching Gracie? Is this the reason why her arms were often swinging in the dark of the night? "The man who attacked you?" Once he finished washing her, he returned the cloth to the bowl, rinsed it, and then settled back onto the pallet, wrapping her in his warm embrace again, hoping she would finish her story.

"Aye. The one who touched me and Gracie."

Even in the dark, he could tell that she was staring off into space as if she were reliving that horrible day. He stroked her arms softly, up and down. How could a lass of eight summers find the strength to attack a man? Ashlyn was indeed a strong woman, one made of an iron will and backbone and a fierce protectiveness.

"I am glad you did. He deserved it. 'Tis dishonorable to touch a bairn in such a way."

"But I think I killed him. I'm a murderer, and I've never told anyone about it." Tears ran down her cheeks.

"Lass, no one would fault you for killing a man who attacked you, but I doubt you killed him. Mayhap you injured him. How old were you at the time?"

"I was eight summers old."

"And what did you stab him with?"

"A small dagger."

"There. That proves my point. A small dagger thrust by a young lass would not do enough damage to kill someone. You may have hurt him, but I doubt you killed him."

"I think I did." Her tears had turned to quiet sobs as she clung to him.

"Why do you think that?"

"Because I caught him by surprise. He had no idea I had awakened."

"But still…you were too young."

"I ran at him, the dagger clutched in both of my hands, and I swung it over my head, aiming for his back…"

"As I said, an eight-year-old would not be able to stab a man's back hard enough to…"

"I took him by surprise when I ran toward him, and I swung as hard as I could…"

Sobs racked her body. "Ashlyn, calm down. I'm sure you did not kill him."

"He turned around so fast that I could not stop."

"And?"

"And I stabbed him right through his eye."

# CHAPTER THIRTEEN

She screamed and gripped him like she'd never let go. That horrible night had happened so long ago, but she'd never told anyone about it before. She'd felt the knife plunge into something soft, and warm fluid had run out. The night had been dark, however, so she had no idea what color it had been.

He had screamed and let go of Gracie, who'd started crying as soon as she got a good look at him.

Magnus persisted. "What else? Tell me the rest of it."

She rested her head on his shoulder and continued, clutching his biceps for strength. "He screamed and reached up to his eye. He yelled at me, told me I had blinded him. The dagger fell to the ground, but I could not retrieve it. He ran in circles, cursing me, and I grabbed Gracie and ran off into the deep forest."

"There, you see. You blinded him, and only in one eye, a more than fair punishment for what he had done to both of you."

"But in the morning, he was lying face down on the ground...not moving."

"Are you sure 'twas the same man? Do not forget how dark it was."

"It had to be him. Who else would it have been?"

"Ash, you said the Norse came ashore and burned the houses, attacking the Scots. There had to be other dead bodies there."

She pulled back to gaze into his eyes. Hope blossomed inside her. "You are correct. There were other bodies. I saw them when Robbie came along. Some of his men were burying them." Just like that, Magnus had given her a shred of doubt to hang on to.

"But the others were in the same area," Ashlyn continued, thinking out loud. "He was not. This man lay face down..."

"Then how could you see his face?"

"I could not."

"Then how do you know it was him?"

"Because…" She pulled back and gazed into his eyes. "Because he was close to the same place…"

"The man you just told me about would have run off. He was strong enough to scream and move around, then he would *not* have stayed in that same spot. It must have been a dead body from the skirmish. You were so distraught that you did not notice the body before in the dark."

She closed her eyes. His reasoning making sense to her adult mind, but for so long she'd viewed the events of that night through the haze of childish fears.

Mayhap she had it all wrong. Mayhap her eight-year-old mind had been so frightened that she hadn't seen the situation clearly. She threw her arms around him and said, "Many thanks, Magnus."

"You never saw the face of the dead man, so you understand there is no way you could know it was the same man, aye?"

"Aye." A few more tears squeaked out. "I did not see it before, but now I understand."

"My sweet, you have carried this too long, for no reason," he said, brushing a kiss on her forehead. "I'll remind you that many of your clanmates have killed to protect others. If you had killed him, it was to defend your sister. No one would judge you for this. Have you never told your mother?"

She shook her head.

"Why not?"

"I was afraid. I thought I was a murderer. I thought…" She shook her head as her gaze locked on his. "But you are correct. I have killed and maimed others and I carry no guilt for it. They were attacking us. I guess being a child…"

"Hush. Remove it from your mind. I tell you now that you were not large enough to have possessed the force to kill that man. He ran off. You injured him to save your sister, 'tis commendable. You should only have pride for what happened."

There was a new lightness inside her as she rested her head on his shoulder. Fear and guilt had tormented her for much too long.

He brushed a tear from her cheek. "Then 'tis time to sleep. Close your eyes and I promise to keep you warm. This has been a long, difficult day, though it ended quite pleasantly." He kissed her cheek and then tugged her close to him.

She lay awake for a while longer, listening to Magnus's rhythmic breathing, enjoying the warmth he gave her and the feeling of being protected. She'd had no idea their relationship would come to this.

Now she understood a wee bit better why her mother, Aunt Gwyneth, and Aline had found it in them to marry. Her life had changed forever, and she found herself reflecting on Magnus's sweet words—*he loves me, he loves me*—as she fell into a blissful sleep.

By the time she woke up, the sun was almost at its highest point. The first thing she did was grab the plaid and tuck it around her because she was shivering. Magnus stood by the hearth, loading more wood and tending to the fire. She sat up and brushed the sleep out of her eyes, wondering if she had dreamed all that had happened.

Magnus gave her a wide smile and strode over to kiss her, which told her she had not imagined any of it. "How do you fare this morn, Ash? You are not too sore, are you?" He moved back to the fire and brought her a warm bowl of broth he'd made with some of the turnips and carrots.

"How long have you been awake?" She sipped the broth, enjoying the warmth as it traveled through her bones.

"A couple of hours. The snow has ended, the sky is lightening up, and the sun may peek out for a wee bit."

"We can leave? I can be ready in a short time."

"Actually, the snow is deep. If the sun comes out, it may melt quite a bit, so I think we should wait until the morrow to leave. 'Twill be better for the horses if they do not have to track through such heavy snow. Do you not agree?"

She stood up, the plaid still wrapped around her bare body, and set the bowl on the table. Her trews were on the stool, so she picked them up and stared at Magnus, waiting for him to give her some privacy.

When he didn't move, instead staring at her with that ever-present grin on his face, she said, "Turn around, please?"

The grin grew wider, all of his white teeth now showing. "Are you to deny me a simple pleasure this morn? You are a beautiful woman."

She frowned at him, swirling her finger in a circular pattern. "Nay, you are dressed, and I did not watch you do it."

He addressed her over his shoulder as he turned. "I do not mind if you watch me."

"You would not let me watch you last night." She stepped into her trews as fast as she could before she donned her shift and wool gown.

"Och, you may watch all you like. 'Tis the studying I do not favor."

She had to chuckle at that one. The man had a way about him that made her feel special. The day suddenly looked brighter.

Then she remembered. Her voice came out in a low whisper as she stared at the fire in the hearth. "I told you, did I not, Magnus?"

"About the man you stabbed? Aye, you did. Now you can remove it from your memory. You are not a murderer."

Aye, he had convinced her that it was possible the man on the ground had been someone else. The feeling of freedom washed over her again, stronger even than last night, and she returned his grin. Striding over, she kissed him on the mouth and announced, "Shall we not go outside, see if we can find a duck or a pheasant?"

"Aye. But not until I get a taste of you. If not with my eyes, then…" He cupped her face and kissed her, stroking her until she opened for him and leaned against him, her arms moving up to his shoulders.

When he ended the kiss, he teased her even more. "Och, you did learn something last eve."

She swatted his shoulder, and he grabbed her mantle, helping her on with it. "You take care of your needs first. I shall follow in a few minutes after I've slowed the fire. I made a path for you, lass."

As soon as she stepped outside, she found the path he'd made. It led behind a couple of trees—the perfect spot to complete her ablutions, which included throwing some cold snow on her face to wash it. It was freezing, but it felt good to remove the day's grime. She had the most wonderful memories of her night with Magnus, and did not regret any of it. Her mother would tell her they needed to marry right away, but she was not sure what would happen. They were both older, and he was a widower. Her head told her it was not necessary as long as she was not carrying, but her heart reminded her that she could have what she'd always wished for. She could marry Magnus and have the family she'd always wanted. They had already discussed marriage, but she hadn't known if she could complete the act. Now that she had, it changed everything. But was it fair to him to marry him if she could not return his love? She'd have to raise the topic with Magnus before they arrived on Grant land.

But that was a few days away. For today, she would simply enjoy his company and their freedom. And mayhap they'd have the opportunity to explore each other again. Her cheeks burned when the cottage's door opened and Magnus stepped out.

Hellfire, but when had he turned so handsome? His dark hair curled into waves down to his shoulders. He usually kept it shorter, but he'd been traveling lately, so probably hadn't thought of it. She had to admit she liked it longer. His beard had been growing for a few days, but even that had grown attractive to her.

Magnus's body was also a thing of beauty, she realized as she watched him lead the horses out of their enclosure. In fact, she decided to give his body her full attention today. Why not enjoy it while she could? No one would see her staring, enjoying the rippling of his muscles, so she decided to take advantage of their present freedom.

"What are you thinking about? 'Tis quite an expression you have on your face. Do I dare ask?"

She decided to goad him. "I was thinking about your cock again."

He coughed once, but then regained his smile. "And are they pleasant thoughts, lass? I can promise you a view of it later, if you'd like. 'Tis not too enticing to look at in the cold. It shrivels and shrinks like a turtle in its shell. 'Twas not too easy washing it earlier because of the temperature."

She burst into hysterics over that, laughing so hard that tears came to her eyes.

He ignored her and said, "Here's your bow and quiver." After giving her some time to get everything situated, he leaned over her shoulder from behind her and whispered into her ear, "I can play your game, too, if you'd like. I'd wager I can shock you more than you can shock me."

She narrowed her gaze and said, "Sounds like an entertaining day. Shall we go?"

He helped her mount her horse, and once they were both astride he followed her into the meadow. She found an area at the top of a hill and reined in her horse.

Magnus stopped his horse next to hers and said, "Now if I could just get you to ride me like you ride that horse."

She fell off her horse.

"Ash," he jumped off his horse. "Are you all right? I did not mean to cause you harm."

She was flat on her back, and he bent over to help her up. Once in a sitting position, she winked at him and said, "My foot was caught." She held her hands up to him and said, "Here, help me up." She waited until he stood in front of her, then looked at his male parts and said, "Hmmm. I wonder...The lassies in the kitchens told me about their mouths and a man's..."

"All right." He spun on his heel. "I yield. No more of that, or I'll not be able to ride home. Hellfire." He glanced over his shoulder at her. "I thought you were an innocent."

"Looking for another snowbank?" She stood up, brushed the snow off her trews, and then slid up behind him and rested her chin on his shoulder. "I have little experience, but that does not mean I do not like to listen. You can learn much that way, and I have many male cousins."

He turned around and took her in his arms. "So you do, and I concede to you. That game causes me too much torture."

"'Tis just as well. I did not have much else to say." There was a faint rustling sound above, and she tipped her head toward the sky and turned to her right just in time to see couple of pheasants near the trees. Stepping away from Magnus, she nocked an arrow, squared herself and took aim, though it took two arrows to take one down.

"Wonderful! Meat for dinner again!" Magnus ran toward the bird, but then stopped at the top of the hill. "It landed at the bottom. The snow is deep on the hill. I'll go get it. You stay here."

"Nay, we'll both go get it." When she reached the hill, she lay down on top of the snow, putting her arms over her head. "We'll roll down."

He laughed as she started down the hill. "Wait for me," he yelled. "We could have raced."

Their laughter echoed through the trees as they propelled down the steep hill. To their mutual surprise, he landed on top of her at the base of the hill.

"Now this is the heavens telling us something, lass."

"What are they telling us?" She peered into his brown eyes, almost the same color as hers, but his held a fleck of gold that matched his smile. Lying on the snow was nice because his weight did not crush her. Hellfire, but she had the sudden urge to kiss him and feel him inside her again. Would it be as nice today?

"This." He settled his lips on hers.

His lips were cold, but the rest of him was sheer delight. His heat radiated to every part of her skin, heating her in ways she could not have fathomed before last night. She parted her lips for him, wanting to taste her Magnus.

His lips trailed a path across her cheek and down her neck. "I say we grab the pheasant and go back."

"Why?" Her question came out in a breathy huff.

"So I can sate your needs where it's warm."

"You think I have needs?"

"Aye, I know you do."

"And what are they?" She ran her fingers through the tendrils of his hair flying everywhere, wet from the snow.

"You need me inside you. You were thinking about it not long ago." He pushed her scarf up so he could nuzzle her ear, flicking the sensitive skin with his tongue as he laughed.

"And how would you know that?" She tipped her head back, giving him better access to her neck.

"I could see your nipples peak through your clothing."

"Nay, you could not."

"Tell it true …you were thinking about me, were you not?"

"Aye, I was…" She sighed as his tongue traveled down her chest, moving fabric aside to clear his trail.

He chuckled, almost finding his way to her nipple, but too much clothing interfered.

"Aye."

"Aye, what?" He stopped his teasing and gazed into her eyes.

"Aye, let's go back. I do want you inside me, but where it's warm, not here."

He pushed himself away from her, then helped her to his feet.

Bending over, he chewed on her lower lip just a bit.

"The pheasant," she reminded him through a laugh.

He looked around for a moment before spotting it. Almost tripping in his haste, he ran to retrieve the bird. Soon they were climbing up the hill again. Her mind was so befuddled by desire as Magnus helped her onto her horse that she would not have been able to find the way back to the hut by herself.

# CHAPTER FOURTEEN

Magnus did his best to calm the fire in his blood, at least until they arrived back at the hut. Hellfire, he had almost taken the lass out in the middle of a snowbank. What had she done to his brain? Once they reached the warmth of their temporary home, he tossed the pheasant into a snowbank by the door where he could tend to it later.

After he made sweet love to Ashlyn again. Neither had said much on the ride back. He was too busy trying to calm his need…a need that had been sated last night like never before.

Yet it was even stronger this morn. He wanted her again, wanted to touch those luscious curves that fit so perfectly in his hands. Ashlyn was different from the other lasses in their clan. She was fierce of spirit, and there was little delicate about her other than her skin. He came up behind her in the hut, caressing her bottom from behind. "Will your tender sensibilities survive the light of day, Ashlyn?"

She spun around and gazed up at him. "Aye. I am still curious, wondering if 'twill be the same today." Her gaze carried a flicker of hope—one he wished to fan into a wild blaze.

"Allow me to attend to the fire, then I'll assist you in doffing your clothing."

"Mayhap I'll assist you with *your* clothing."

He chuckled as he tossed his mantle to the side and then bent down to take care of the fire. When he finished, he stood to face her. The sight before him froze him in his spot. There she stood with naught on.

"You take my breath away." He'd made sure to warm his hands over the fire before he stood. He removed his clothing, setting it all on the stool before he moved to take her into his arms.

She whispered, "Will you not show me?

"Show you what? I'll show you whate'er you'd like."

"Show me how to ride you like a horse."

"Aye. With pleasure. You shall be pleased to be on top, I think. But first allow me the opportunity to relish you and your curves the way they deserve to be worshipped."

He kissed her lips tenderly, groaning into her mouth when her nipples hardened against him. He tugged on her lower lip, nipping her just a touch, and she opened for him, allowing him into her sweetness. His tongue slowly penetrated her mouth, taunting and tasting her, stroking her until a small sound at the back of her throat told him that her need was building as much as his.

They explored each other, his hand cupping the soft globes of her bottom while her delicate hands skimmed down his back until they rested on his hips. He carried her to the pallet, their lips still locked until he settled her underneath him. Her gaze was filled with trust, and she had no idea how that trust unmanned him. She was so beautiful, so enticing, every inch of her lovely flesh tempting him to pound into her for his own needs. But he would not. He cared more about her pleasure than he did about his own.

Her breasts skimmed against his chest in a light tease, and he settled on his side, facing her. His hands caressed her hips and followed a trail up to her breasts. He massaged one, gently tweaking the responsive peak. His gaze caught hers, and he enjoyed watching her respond to his touch. Leaning down, he took the succulent peak into his mouth, lazily tracing a path around the base of her nipple until her hands laced through his hair, gripping him with pleasure. He took her full in his mouth, drawing the tip in and releasing it in a rhythm he knew she felt because her ragged breathing matched his.

He slipped his erection between her thighs, and she responded by spreading her legs for him, giving him access to her passage. His hand wove through her curls until he found her sleek folds. Then he slipped a finger inside her, and her heat wrapped around his finger, making him groan.

"Show me, Magnus. Show me how to ride you." Her hand cupped his face and she kissed him, a gentle tease that almost slayed him. She was so honest with her feelings, with her sensuality. He shifted her on top of him, guiding her legs on either side of him so that she was straddling him.

Her eyes widened and she her mouth formed a full circle. "Oh."

"Aye. You have me right where you want me. I am all yours, but trust me, lass—" his voice came out in husky pants, "—I cannot wait much longer."

She squirmed and wiggled until she was directly above his cock. He reached up and cupped her breasts, fondling her nipples as she reached down and wrapped her hand around his cock. Moaning with delight, she brought her hand up and down his length a few times before she centered herself over him, carefully placing his cock where she wanted him. Then she plunged down slowly, allowing herself time to adjust to him.

When he was buried to the hilt in her hot sheath, he groaned, his hands switching to her hips so he could help guide her with her movement. She rocked against him, awkward at first until she found her rhythm, her breathing telling him she was not far from climaxing. She opened her eyes to look at him. "Magnus, is this good for you?"

"Aye." Good? Shite, she rode him so well he could barely speak. As she continued to slide down and back, down and back, she spread her legs so he could penetrate her deeper, bringing him inside so far that he felt like he'd died and gone to heaven.

Her hands glided up his body, stopping at his nipples, then she leaned down to raze her teeth over each one.

"Ash, do not play much longer."

She splayed her hands across his chest for leverage and rammed him hard, unwavering in her pressure and rhythm, her need driving her into a frenzy that almost sent him over the edge. But he would not go over without her. He held his breath and massaged her sex until she screamed his name, convulsing on him. His seed shot into her, and he felt his world dim under the force of his pleasure. She collapsed on top of him, her face nuzzled into his neck.

Neither spoke until they regained their control. Magnus brought his hand up behind her back, tucking her close. Making love with her was unbelievable, like naught he'd ever experienced. Who would have believed that the lass who preferred to be prickly with every man she met was truly as sweet as any could possibly be?

When he was finally able to speak, he whispered, "Did you like riding me, lass?"

She giggled, rolling off him to his side. "Aye. Magnus, I have a feeling there are many other things you can teach me."

He grinned.

Ashlyn lifted her newly plaited hair off her neck, thinking about how wonderful Magnus's hands had felt the night before. How she wished he would manage her hair every day. They were outside now, preparing to continue with their journey. They hoped to take advantage of the weather and travel the entire day. The sky was clear, and the air temperature had warmed a wee bit.

Magnus readied her horse for her, and when he helped her mount, he said, "A part of me wishes to stay here forever."

She had to admit she'd been thinking the same thing. "I agree. Our time together has been wonderful. I must thank you for being so kind and patient."

"Ash, I never expected to fall in love with you, and I never expected to be blessed with such a wonderful two days alone with you. I have to admit it was more than I ever thought it would be." He paused. "I feel I need to remind you that you gave me your maidenhead. 'Twas a most wondrous gift, and the teachings of my sire and my laird tell me that we should marry. If 'tis what you wish, I will honor it."

Somehow, his offer of marriage did not sound as enthusiastic as she'd hoped to hear, his declaration being that they *should* marry, not that he wished to marry. She decided to be honest with him. "I am more confused than ever. I had not expected our time together to be so enjoyable, but I cannot swear my love for you. Is that fair?" His brief mention of falling in love had not been heartwarming or convincing. Had he changed his mind? Had she disappointed him in some way?

"Mayhap we are rushing this."

"Mayhap we just need to spend more time together, especially at home. Much has happened in a short time, Magnus, and I must thank you for your support, but I need to work things through in my mind."

Magnus nodded and mounted his horse, and they traveled in silence for quite a ways, both lost in their thoughts. The day was beautiful, but Ashlyn's mind was troubled. Should she not wish that Magnus would swear his undying love for her, that he should wish to marry immediately? Instead, she felt almost…relieved. Finally, she realized what was holding her back.

Fear. The fear of disappointing him. The fear that he might leave her. She was not like Rhona at all. His first wife had been so sweet, and sweet was never a word anyone would use to describe her. She wished to give her heart to him, but what if she wasn't enough for him? Was his reluctance because he was not ready give his heart to someone else? Was he missing his wife even more?

She could not get rid of the fear of being left behind. It had happened to her too many times. Her father had left her and her mother when he had drowned in the boat. Others had come and gone after that. True, one man had stayed with them for much longer than the rest, and they'd all hated him, but there had been others who had stayed for a short time and then left. Ashlyn had almost loved one of them the way she had loved her da, but he had left and never returned.

The experience that had hurt the most, though, was that awful night after Robbie Grant had taken her mother away. She'd thought she and Gracie would be alone forever. Then that wicked man had come and hurt them. It had been the start of several days of terror, but eventually Robbie had found them and he'd sent her and Gracie into the Highlands, a place they had never been before. Again, she had felt abandoned, even though they'd made the trip with their wonderful escorts, Logan and Gwyneth. She recalled wondering if she'd ever see her mother again.

That feeling of being abandoned had drilled down to her very bones.

She couldn't bear ever being abandoned again, by a husband or by anyone.

So she had never allowed anyone close enough to hurt her.

# CHAPTER FIFTEEN

Magnus saw something out of the corner of his eye and brought his mount to a stop. The sun was not yet at its highest, and while it had melted some of the snow, the ground was still covered in at least one hand's length.

"What is it, Magnus?" Ashlyn peered past him to see what had caught his eye.

He led his horse over to the heap buried in the snow, dismounting when he came abreast of it. "I pray 'tis not a dead body."

He brushed some of the snow off the pile.

"I think 'tis an animal, not a person."

He knelt down beside it. "Aye, 'tis a deer." He brushed the snow off to get a better look.

"Is that an arrow?" Ashlyn asked.

"Aye."

Ashlyn's head jerked up to scan the area. "How odd. I do not recall the carcass being there on the way down, so it must have happened after the snowfall."

"It looks like the breast was cut away for someone's dinner. We must have company not far from here, but it would surprise me if they were reivers. They usually do not travel about in the snow."

"We shall have to test our tracking skills," Ashlyn said.

Magnus mounted his horse. "I hope your skills are better than mine."

"Aye, Uncle Logan trained me. We need to head toward the sun so I can look for ridges left by horses."

"But there's too much snow to show hoof prints."

"Aye, 'tis true, but tracks may show in ravines or shallow areas near rocks, and the uneven ground should show in the sunlight."

Magnus shrugged his shoulders and let her take the lead. It was not long before Ashlyn had settled into her warrior countenance, her attention completely devoted to her task.

A couple of hours later, she pointed ahead of them, her face breaking into a huge smile. "Look, Magnus. Do you see it? 'Tis not just one horse but several, and the paths all lead in the same direction."

If they hadn't taken the time to track the hunters, they would have missed the smoke off in the distance. There was also a new path that he did not recall seeing on the way to Edinburgh.

"Ash, do you recall that path?" he asked, pointing.

"Nay, we did not see aught from here until the big ravine. I recall Jamie telling us there's a keep there that has been deserted for two years. The walls are crumbling."

They stared over the land, neither saying a word until Ashlyn whispered, "We must go see who it is."

Magnus stopped his horse and dismounted. "Why? We have no idea who that is. 'Tis not hard to believe that someone would inhabit the place in winter, just as we did. Mayhap they are simply holing up during the storm."

"But what if..." She held her arms out to him and he assisted her down.

"What? What is running through your mind?" He turned, his hands on his hips, afraid of what she was about to say.

"What if 'tis Ranulf?"

He could hear the raw emotion in her voice. The possibility she raised had been in the back of his mind, but he'd ignored it intentionally. He did not wish to risk Ashlyn's life. "I agreed to see if there was someone there, but I never agreed to attempt to stop MacNiven with just the two of us. Ash, 'tis a huge risk I am not ready to take. We cannot go there. We are alone. If you're correct, what are our chances? 'Twill be two against how many?"

"We cannot just leave without checking. We must." She tugged on his hand for emphasis.

"We'll go back for assistance first. We're closer to Grant land than Edinburgh. There should be guards patrolling not far from here."

"We cannot take that chance, Magnus. What if they leave?"

He wrapped both his hands around her wee one. Hellfire, but he admired her bravery. Still, he could not risk her safety. What if...

She moved over so their sides touched. "I see how your mind is working. You mustn't let your worry for me sway you. Do you not recall our king's edict? He wants MacNiven found. That could be him."

Magnus ran his hand across the top of his head, rubbing his hair, wishing some solution would pop into his mind, but it did not. "I cannot risk it."

"Then I shall go on my own." She tugged on the reins of her horse.

He stopped her. "Nay, you'll not go on your own."

"We were given a task to complete by our king, and there is a fair chance that task is across that meadow," she snapped. "How can you leave with a clear conscience?"

"All right. Please think on this. We cannot go charging in there as though we are one hundred guards or more, but if you insist, we shall get close enough to determine who has inhabited the ruins. Please remember, my sweet, that chances are they are reivers who have come in from the cold for a couple of nights. If it proves to be MacNiven, you must agree that if there are more than two guards there, we will head to Grant land for assistance before we attempt to take on a group that vastly outnumbers us. Agreed?"

He watched her work this through in her mind. The poor lass wanted the lout to be held accountable for all he'd done. Could he blame her? "Ashlyn? I'll have your agreement before we move any closer. I will not take us into a bloodbath. Please tell me you recall that battle at Castle Dubh and all the dead."

That comment hit home, he could tell.

She stared at her hands for a moment, but then whispered, "I agree. But do you not agree with me that we should at least observe? Find out what we can?"

"Aye. I can accept that, as long as you promise not to attack someone on your own. You are verra good with your bow and arrow, but not so good with your fists."

"Accepted."

"You promise to stay by my side?"

"Aye."

Magnus searched the area. "We'll secure the horses in that

circle of trees, then move closer on foot. Please follow my lead, lass. We do not wish to draw attention to ourselves. I do have more experience in that area than you do. Remember Edinburgh."

"I'll follow you."

She agreed too quickly. His hands settled on her waist and he gave her a light squeeze before he lifted her onto her horse. Hellfire, but he hoped it was not MacNiven. She might go charging at the fool without thinking. There was too much emotion involved.

Ashlyn's heart beat so strong she looked at her chest to see if she could see it, but fortunately, she could not. She stayed behind him as she'd promised, vowing to herself that she'd follow his instructions and not act as rashly as she had done in Edinburgh.

Once they reached the trees, he placed his hands on her waist and lifted her off her horse without making a sound. Throwing the reins over bushes, he took her hand and led her toward the back of the crumbling curtain wall. With any luck, they would find a break in the back.

She had to admit that walking hand-in-hand was a welcome intimacy. And she could not deny that she liked the way he looked at her—as though he cared.

He'd said he loved her, and she realized she was ready to admit that she felt the same way. This would be a foolish time, but mayhap she could tell him tonight when they were alone. He was her protector, her lover, and the only person who knew all of her shortcomings and fears.

Magnus did his best to trek through the areas where the snow had already melted, somehow able to find those few areas without much effort to be certain they did not leave a trail of footprints. When they reached the edge of the curtain wall, he turned around with his finger to his lips, indicating he'd heard something and she needed to be quiet.

She clutched his arm and listened.

A female voice spoke first. "Do you like warming his bed?"

A second female voice answered. "Aye. 'Tis what I must do if I wish to stay around."

"You think he will get rid of us?"

"Nay. He told me he needs us both in Edinburgh. He feels

justice was not served correctly, and he plans to right it. I do not know how, but he is cunning and devious. He promised me much coin if we do our job right."

"But what job?"

"I know not, but mayhap if he pays us enough coin, we can find our own place to live. He talks as though he only plans to be in Edinburgh for a short while."

"One of his guards told me there are large bordellos in Edinburgh where women get paid a portion of the money they make for spreading their legs."

"If he doesn't pay us for the job he wants done, mayhap I'll do that," the woman said with a heavy sigh.

"And what would you do if we stay in Edinburgh?"

"I do not know. I did not ask for this life, and I'm already tired of it. I'd like to be married and have bairns, but I do not think 'twill ever happen now."

The other lass sighed. "Aye, 'tis the way of the world. At least our chief treats us better than Hew Gordon treated Aline."

Ashlyn squeezed Magnus's hand. Aye, they'd found MacNiven—together. He turned to her and gave her a quick kiss on her lips.

The first voice spoke again. "I'm getting cold. I wish to return to the keep. I hate this building, 'tis too drafty, and there are not enough men to keep wood in the hearth."

"We may not be here long. The chief is awaiting confirmation of something. I know he has plans to move to a nice keep, though I know not where. I hope he keeps us both. I'll return to the keep with you. Promise not to say a word of what I've shared?"

"I promise."

There was a loud rustling of skirts as the women trudged back through leaves and snow toward the great hall.

"What do we do?" Ashlyn whispered in Magnus's ear.

"We go get assistance, as I said before."

"But we know not how many are here. She said there were not enough guards to cut wood. Would it not help the Grant guards to know how many are here?"

"Aye, you have a point." He released her hand and crept down the wall to another opening, but then came back to her.

He pointed to the spot he had just come from. "I'll use that opening to get inside because 'tis near the back entrance to the kitchens and the hall. I'll wait there a few minutes to see if I can learn aught or see any guards. You are to stay here and do naught."

Her eyes widened.

"Ashlyn, promise me you will not run off like a daft woman."

"But can I not go with you?"

"Believe me, I would rather keep you within sight, but we will be easily seen if we travel together inside the wall. 'Tis safer for you to stay here. I hope to only be a few minutes. If the guards are around, I shall know right away if we are outnumbered."

She scowled, but he lifted her chin with his finger.

"Promise me? I cannot bear to think about anything happening to you."

She hated to do it, but she nodded.

"Good. Have your bow and arrow ready." He tugged her to him and kissed her forehead, then gave her a sound kiss on the lips. He whispered, "I love you."

Off he went toward the opening before she had the opportunity to tell him how she felt. Aye, her love for him had blossomed, and she was delighted. Now she needed to let him know. How she wished to follow him, but she had given him her word. After the incident in Edinburgh, she did not want to risk going off on her own.

Waiting for Magnus would feel like an eternity.

# CHAPTER SIXTEEN

Magnus crept inside the crumbling wall as soon as he was certain he was the only one in the surrounding area. Once inside, he concealed himself in a cluster of bushes, hopeful that he might overhear something useful.

He could be patient. He just prayed that Ashlyn could do the same. He held his breath as soon as a side door opened, waiting to see who came through. Three men moved out, and he tuned in to their conversation as best he could. He heard bits and pieces.

"Meet in front….to update us."

"When do we leave?"

"Not sure… We're probably about to find out."

Magnus watched them as they moved toward the front of the keep. He didn't have enough information yet. While he recognized the best plan would be to move into hearing distance of the group, he recalled Jake's teasing words about his size. The only other thing that he could hide behind was the eight-foot tall curtain wall.

He scowled, wishing he were as small as Kenzie or as fast as Loki. Jake was almost as big as he was, but there was something about Magnus's physique that drew the eye. Hellfire, he had to try. Glancing around, he saw no one, so he crept up to a smaller group of trees and bushes, hoping to hide inside them.

He was there for less than five minutes when he heard the chuckles of a guard behind him. Spinning on his heel, he drew his sword. There were four guards headed toward him, all with swords drawn and aimed at his midsection.

Magnus did not wait for them to reach him. He went at them swinging hard, his sword coming from every direction possible. He killed the first guard with one stroke, catching him in his neck vessel. Blood shot everywhere before he fell to the ground. With the same stroke, Magnus managed to slow another one with a hit to his belly. He swung his sword arm over his head and down in an oblique line, catching the third guard in his middle.

That left the fourth guard, who stared at him transfixed. As soon as Magnus lifted his sword, he could see the fear in his enemy's eyes. He thrust his sword into the fool's heart, killing him instantly. Jake had told him these guards lacked in skill, and he saw that it was true.

But Magnus had made one mistake—he had forgotten about the second guard. He'd pulled his sword out of the last victim and was stooping to wipe it clean in the snow when he noticed the second guard had propped himself up on one knee and extended his arm. Magnus cut him down quickly, but not before the bastard caught him across his thigh with his sword, slicing his flesh open.

This time he checked all four before he checked his leg. All were dead. The wound stung like hell, which worried him a bit. Normally he could ignore wounds, but this one felt a bit deeper. He decided to head back to the open spot he'd used to breach the wall—surely he'd be caught now—but a noise behind him forced him to spin around, his sword already raised overhead in preparation to attack.

Too late. His movements had slowed enough for him to be caught. Six men raced toward him, all poised to strike, but a voice rang out across the open area. "Not yet!"

The men fell in around him, surrounding him, and he dropped his sword on the ground, gathering his strength. He knew it was hopeless taking on six men with swords. He'd rather fight that many with his fists. Since he knew they were MacNiven's men, it was better to survive now and fight later. Every move he made now needed to be to protect Ashlyn. She was not far from them on the other side of the wall. He prayed she would either stay there or retreat.

The man who came forward was wearing a helm. "Hold him, I want him alive." He moved right up to Magnus and whispered, "I know that plaid. A Grant, are you? Where are your friends?" He recognized the man as MacNiven.

Another guard said, "Hellfire. If he's a Grant…" He turned in a circle, scanning the trees for something. "Beware, they often travel with archers."

"And my clan will be here any moment," Magnus sneered, "and there'll be archers and swordsman everywhere." How he wished it were true. His thinking had turned a bit hazy. He noticed fresh blood continued to stain his trews, and sweat dotted his brow despite the cold.

"Is that so? Where are they now? How many?" the helmed man asked.

"MacNiven, they'll be everywhere soon."

Just as he made that declaration, two arrows came out of nowhere, one catching a guard in his eye, and the other hitting the guard to the right of Magnus in his chest, dropping him to the ground.

Ashlyn heard yelling and the sound of swords in battle, so she crept over to the opening in the wall to peek through. She prayed MacNiven's men were merely practicing, but something told her that Magnus might be in trouble.

If so, it would be all her fault. He had been level headed enough to suggest they go to Grant land for help; she had talked him out of it. The sounds were clearer once she reached the hole in the curtain wall, but she could not tell who was involved or exactly what was transpiring. There were four men on the ground, and several others were running toward the skirmish.

Magnus.

It had to be Magnus they were running toward. She readied her bow and pulled an arrow out of her quiver, but she could not get a clear shot from where she stood. Other than marching out into the middle of the opening, where she would be seen right away, there was no way for her to get a clear shot. Her gaze traveled up to the top of the curtain wall, but it looked unsteady, and the rocks were crumbling in many places.

Then finally she saw it. There was a huge oak tree a wee distance away. Even though the season had stripped it of its leaves, there were two pine trees next to it that would hide her somewhat.

She had to take the risk. Climbing up the tree, she almost yelled when she lost her balance and tore the skin off her wrist on the rough bark, but she kept control and carried on. Magnus was counting on her, and the only way she could help him was with her bow and arrow. Tears threatened to blur her vision as soon as she stopped climbing and absorbed the situation that was unfolding beneath her. There were several guards surrounding Magnus, and one of them wore a helm. MacNiven.

She caught some words about the Grant plaid, so she knew she did not have much time. Propping herself up as best she could, she nocked her arrow, aimed it, and let it fly, catching one of the guards right square in his eye. Without pausing, she nocked another arrow and caught a second guard in the chest. Both dropped to the ground.

MacNiven turned to flee, shouting instructions at his guards. "Kill him. Then we're leaving. We need to get out of here before the rest of the Grants arrive. No more battles. I cannot afford to lose any of you. Donal, get the women."

One guard pulled his sword out, but Ashlyn shot him in the belly before he could take one more step toward Magnus. MacNiven ran in the opposite direction from where Ashlyn sat, so she aimed quick and let her arrow loose, pleased to see it connect with his shoulder.

All the others rushed after MacNiven except for Magnus, who started limping toward the curtain wall.

MacNiven was getting away, so she grabbed another arrow, nocked it, and let it fly, but she missed. She was reaching for another when everything changed. One of the men running away with MacNiven changed his path and ran straight for Magnus.

Magnus was badly hurt, and he was in no condition to spar with the man who was headed his way. But MacNiven's man had a short distance to go before he would reach Magnus. It might be enough for her to fire one more arrow at MacNiven. Reaching for another arrow from her quiver, she turned back toward MacNiven. But from the corner of her eye she saw Magnus stumble. A fall could be fatal; his attacker would be upon him in but a moment. She glanced back at MacNiven, who was almost too far for her arrows to find their target. If she helped Magnus, the blackguard would be gone. She'd have no chance of repaying him for all the trouble he'd caused—all the men who had died because of him and all the women who had been mistreated.

She had to make a choice, and she found it easy.

Magnus.

Under no circumstances could she allow MacNiven's man to hurt Magnus. She swiveled her bow toward the man who was rushing toward Magnus. She let the arrow fly and hit the lout in his heart, dropping him instantly. As soon as she was sure he was not moving, she slid down the tree and ran hard for the opening in the curtain wall.

"Magnus, are you hale? What happened? What is wrong?" She was almost upon him when she noticed the amount of blood on his trews. Fear shot through her. "Oh my, look at the blood. I must get you to my mother. You'll need stitching, cleaning, and poultices."

When she reached his side, he wrapped his arm over her shoulder. His face was pale, but he looked alert. "Ash, get my horse. I may not be able to get myself up on him if we wait much longer." She saw the problem in an instant. It would be physically impossible for her to lift him onto the animal. He had to be able to assist.

They made their way through the curtain wall, and then Magnus gave her a wee push. "Go. Get my horse. Do not worry about them; they are on the run. He only has a few men left and he's taking them with him."

"Magnus, I'm so sorry. This is all my fault."

"Nay, lass. You did not take a sword to me. I should not have tried to hide in the bushes. Jake has told me for years that I am too big to conceal myself. It does not help that I always pick the wrong places. Now go. Please go, and do not slow."

As she took off to retrieve his horse, she yelled back over her shoulder. "You are bleeding too much. My mother always says to press down on your wound to get the blood to stop. Try it, please, while I get your horse."

Praying she could get the beasts back to the curtain wall in time, she ran even faster.

When she returned, she could tell by his color that he was not doing well. "Magnus?" She noticed he was pushing on his wound.

"Aye?" He glanced up at her.

"I need to say something, and then we shall get you home. I love you, and I'm quite pleased that you love me. Now, see if you can mount and I'll help you if you've need of it."

His beautiful smile lit up his face. "That pleases me. I'll make it home for you, Ash." He gave her a quick kiss, then managed to get up on the horse, though she had to steady him to keep him from falling off the other side.

"Mayhap I should ride with you, give you something to hang on to?"

"I weigh so much more than you that I fear I would pull you off with me. Besides, the horses will travel faster with a lighter load. If I cannot hold myself up, I'll lay across the horse. He'll get me home." The horse whinnied in response, nodding his head as if he understood. "We have but a day's journey left. I think I can make it."

Ashlyn stood next to his horse and took a moment to check his wound, lifting his hand to see how much it continued to bleed. "I think it has almost stopped, but I wish to pinch it a bit longer. My mama says you must pinch a wound to get it to stop bleeding. Continuous bleeding is what does the most damage. She also says 'tis important to clean a wound, but I cannot get your trews off to do that."

"I put some snow on it while you were gone to get the dirt out. To my surprise, it stemmed the bleeding some. Lass, I think we need to leave. MacNiven is heading south. We are going north. They'll not bother us; as usual, the fool has chosen to run, and he's running exactly where we were hoping he would go. Logan is south along with the rest of our team. Mayhap they will meet along the way."

She guided her horse over to a log so she could stand and mount, then they headed out. The sun was almost at its peak, so they wouldn't make it home before dark, but they would move along as quickly as possible and hope for no delays.

"I think it would be best for you to conserve your strength by not talking, so I'll wait until later to question you." She said a quick prayer that they would get home before he fell off his horse.

Magnus led the way and Ashlyn fell in behind him until they made it to the meadow. Most of the path had already been trampled, and they had hit a few areas that had even less snow than they'd seen further south. They moved their horses to a gallop whenever they could. She said so many prayers, she knew not what else to say.

Dark was almost upon them when she noticed Magnus was having trouble keeping his head up. Now was the time to talk to him, to try to keep him awake. She pulled her horse abreast of him.

"Magnus."

"Aye, love?" He cast a grin at her from the side. "I like saying that."

"And you have no idea how grateful I am to hear it. But tell me what you learned. Was it MacNiven?" She was certain of it, but she needed to keep him awake.

"Aye, 'twas him. I saw his eyes, and he recognized the Grant plaid. He only said that they were leaving. He told his men that he wished to get out before any more Grants arrived."

"The women. I believe they could have been Cedrica and Lorna. Did you see them? Do you think they took them?"

"Aye. I think MacNiven must have taken them, if only so that he'll have two more whom he can stand behind in battle. I heard someone tell Donal to get the women. I think they head south; my guess is for the Buchans." His head leaned forward as his body swayed.

"Magnus!" she yelled. He jerked his head up.

"I prefer for you only to yell my name when you're in my arms, lass."

"Forgive me, but I cannot allow you to fall asleep. You must stay awake. If you fall off your horse, I shan't be able to get you back on it."

"I'll hang on just for you."

"Do you think Glenn lied about knowing that MacNiven is alive?"

"Nay, but MacNiven knows that Buchan hates the Ramsays and the Grants, so he will probably search him out for assistance."

"And Davina is there."

"Aye, Davina fears him, but she also loved him. If he comes to her with open arms, I believe she'll follow him, or at least hide him, either from fear or from love."

"Is your wound still bleeding?"

"Nay, it stopped long ago."

"Does it pain you much?"

"Nay, it has no feeling."

His head dipped down, but she thought he was looking at his wound so she took a moment to glance up at the gray sky. The snow was a bit deeper here, but the horses were plodding along. As soon as she returned her gaze to Magnus, she realized her mistake. He slid off his horse, directly into a snow bank.

"Nay, Magnus, nay." She jumped down from her horse, almost falling, but caught herself in time. Hellfire, what was she to do now?

Kneeling next to him, she shook him. "Magnus." He didn't flinch. Apparently, the snow had prevented any injuries from the fall. Though it looked like the wound in his leg hadn't opened again, she was worried she'd never get him back on the horse.

She searched the area for aught she could use to get him on the horse, but found nothing other than a couple of logs. Perhaps she could tug him onto one and sling his upper body over the horse. But she had to get him there first.

She tied his feet to the back of the horse and led the horse over to the logs. She offered a quick prayer of thanks for the snow, especially because it was hard-packed snow instead of the light, fluffy stuff that had protected Magnus in his fall. If not for the snow, she would never have been able to drag him across the field, so she vowed not to complain when the temperature continued to drop.

Once she untied him, she tried to awaken him, but he would not move. Refusing to give up, she put her hands under his arms and tugged him over to the logs. Her horse was already standing there, having found some greens to munch on around the logs, so she made several attempts to lift him. Then she finally did the only thing she could do.

She sat on the log, pulling him close enough to settle his head in her lap, and she cried. She cried the biggest tears she'd ever cried, hugging him close, kissing his cheeks.

"Magnus, forgive me, but I cannot lift you. I can barely move you at all, but I promise not to leave you. I love you and I'll never leave you. Do you hear me? I swear I will love you forever. You are such a good man." She wiped the tears from her eyes. After all these years of swearing off men, she couldn't believe the irony of the situation. She'd finally fallen in love, but she couldn't enjoy it.

A short time later, when her tears finally dried up, she heard a familiar whooshing sound that echoed through the trees. It came from a wee distance away from them. Though it hurt to leave Magnus, she rushed into the trees.

A Ramsay arrow lay embedded in the tree trunk in front of her. She raced back to her horse, located her bow and arrows, and then shot several into the air in different directions, hoping whoever was out there would notice it just as she had heard the arrow that was now embedded in the tree. She was running back toward the path, traveling in the direction they had just come from, when her gaze caught something that made her jump up and down with glee.

"Uncle Logan, Aunt Gwyneth. Over here. Please. I need your help." She waved her arms until they caught sight of her and hurried to her side.

"Ashlyn? Where's Magnus?" Uncle Logan asked. "I saw the tracks and shot the arrow hoping you would notice it. I did not think there were many others this far in the Highlands after the storm."

"He's wounded." She pointed to the area she'd come from and the two dismounted and followed her to his side.

"We ran into MacNiven and his men. He killed many, but he suffered a bad cut on his leg. He lost quite a bit of blood. He was awake until a short time ago, but then he fell off his horse. I could not get to him in time to help him balance."

They did their best to awaken him, but still no luck.

"We need to get him to Caralyn and to warmth," Aunt Gwyneth said. "Let's lay him right over the horse." The three of them managed to get him into a position that would keep him on the horse.

Uncle Logan hugged Ashlyn and said, "Well done in getting him this far. We are almost on Grant land."

Aunt Gwyneth took her hand and led her over to her horse. "Mount up, my dear," she said, helping her. "We need to get you both home. Your color is not much better than his. You must have been stuck in the storm for a while."

"We found an abandoned hut to stay in," she said. "'Twas cold but we had some wood."

"You are safe now, 'tis what's important."

Once they were on the path, the obvious finally dawned on Ashlyn. "Why are you both here? Has something happened?"

Aunt Gwyneth nodded. "Aye, Molly had a bad feeling about the two of you, and we've found her predictions to be quite accurate. We sent her home because her visions were causing her too much pain. The others traveled back to Clan Ramsay to protect Molly and Sorcha. We'll get MacNiven, but first we must protect ourselves."

Uncle Logan glanced at Aunt Gwyneth. "Appears you are correct, wife. Our eldest daughter is a seer."

# CHAPTER SEVENTEEN

Terrified that Magnus would never wake up, Ashlyn fought tears for the rest of their journey.

As soon as they crossed into Grant land, Uncle Logan said, "Gwyneth, go on ahead. Advise them of Magnus's condition so we can get him care as swiftly as possible. Tell them we shall head to his cottage since it is closer to Caralyn."

Gwyneth took off in a gallop, flying across the field ahead of them.

Ashlyn kept praying silently, desperate to do something, anything, to help him.

Just before the Grant castle came into view, Uncle Logan spoke to her, though his gaze rested on Magnus between them. "I'm detecting a bit of a change in your countenance, lass. Do you wish to share aught with me?"

She managed to choke out, "Nay."

"Before you left Clan Grant, you could barely tolerate Magnus's presence. You no longer feel the same?"

"Nay."

"I will not ask you to tell all, because I know you will need to speak to your laird when we arrive, but I'm sensing strong feelings from you. Is it guilt or true feelings for the man?"

"Both."

"Say no more. Remember one thing, Ashlyn. He's a strong man, and if you've given him a reason to live, he'll be more likely to come back. And a man can love two women. My brother adored both of his wives, so remember your uncle Quade when you wonder about that."

Ashlyn nodded, knowing that she'd fall apart if she spoke. The moon shone bright by the time they arrived at the Grant keep, the reflection off the snow lighting their way as they headed toward the gates. A group of riders came out to greet them, Gwyneth among them.

As they came close, Ashlyn could make out her stepfather and her brother Roddy, along with her cousins Jake and Connor. Home, she was finally home. After all the times she'd hoped to go off as a Grant warrior, she'd discovered the truth. It wasn't as exciting as she'd expected. Her home was here on Grant land, and it was the best place in the world. She had no desire to leave again. Her heart swelled to see her stepsire, her brother, and her cousins. The people she loved most of all were here to greet them and help her get Magnus home. What a fool she'd been! She chastised herself. Why could she not be happy with all that she had here? If she'd not insisted on becoming a warrior, this never would have happened.

"Ashlyn, you are hale?" Robbie asked, his voice heavy with worry.

She nodded. "We must get Magnus to Mama."

"She and Gracie are already at his cottage, getting ready for his arrival. We'll follow so we can get him inside."

They continued on, and a small contingency of guards fell in with them when they were closer to the gates, ready to escort them to Magnus's cottage. They traveled in silence, and Ashlyn did her best to keep her tears inside.

Once they reached the cottage, Ashlyn jumped off her horse and ran in ahead of the men, heading straight for her mother. She threw herself into her mama's arms and pleaded with her, "Please fix him, Mama. Fix him."

Her mother hugged her and then kissed her forehead. "Tell me his injuries."

Ashlyn hugged her sister, who stood by their mama's side, while she talked. "His left thigh. He took a sword there, but it was a while before we could pinch the wound. He bled quite a bit, but he was awake for most of the day."

Gracie squeezed Ashlyn back and then rushed over to hold the front door open. Not knowing what else to do, Ashlyn trailed her mother into the bed chamber. Jake, Connor, Roddy, and Robbie carried Magnus inside the hut and then to the bed chamber. Connor and Roddy moved out of the small chamber as soon as they set down their charge, but Jake and Robbie stayed.

Caralyn issued orders. "Robbie, use your dagger to cut his trews off. I need to see the wound."

"I'll help," Ashlyn said, eager to do something.

"Mayhap you should take care of your needs first? You do not look well, Ashlyn." Her mother bustled around the room while her stepsire started to remove Magnus's clothing. "Gracie can help me."

Gracie, who'd followed the lads into the chamber, stood in the corner, wide-eyed confusion evident on her face. Ashlyn knew why without asking—it was because she'd never acted this way about a man, any man.

"Mama, I'm fine. I'll stay and help. 'Tis my fault this happened to him. Why, if I hadn't insisted on going on the mission, I would not have needed a protector, and this would never have happened."

Uncle Logan stood in the doorway, his hands on his hips. "Niece, we mustn't blame ourselves for aught that happens while we are working to protect our clan. Unless you held the sword that sliced his flesh open, 'twas not your fault. Get past that so we can move forward."

She swiped at the tears fighting to get out and forced herself to nod.

Another voice came from behind her uncle. "He is correct in his assessment, lass. You did not choose him as your protector, I did. The person at fault is the warrior who held the sword that cut him. No one else." Uncle Logan moved aside, and Uncle Alex appeared in the door frame. "Caralyn, when you no longer require her help, please send Ashlyn to me so I can hear about all that transpired. And Ashlyn, well done getting him home."

Uncle Alex moved back into the other room. Robbie, finished with his work, followed him out and closed the door.

Caralyn turned to face Ashlyn. "The wound does not look dirty, but hold it open while I wash it out."

"He said he tried to clean it with snow, though he had his trews on, so 'twas difficult. Why does he not awaken, Mama?"

Ashlyn's mother scrubbed the blood and dirt away, then covered the wound with a poultice. "Probably because of all the bleeding. Men often sleep when they bleed heavy, but 'tis also the end of the day, so I suspect he is tired from fighting. He may wake by morn. There is no fever, but that could still set in in another day or two. Are you sure he has no other injuries? He did not hit his head, did he?"

"Nay, not that I saw."

"Where were you when he took the sword in his leg?"

"I was behind the curtain wall, but when I heard the commotion, I climbed a tree and used my bow. I hit several of the men, and the rest ran."

"And was Magnus still moving at that point?"

"Aye, he walked to the wall, and I fetched his horse and helped him to mount. He rode for most of the day. Then he just fell over."

"He did not hit his head?"

"Nay, he landed on his side in a big snowbank."

"Lasses, hold his leg up so I can bandage him."

Ashlyn and Gracie both did as they were instructed.

"He means more to you that just a protector, does he not, daughter?"

Ashlyn's gaze caught her mother's smile, and she did all she could not to weep uncontrollably. "Aye, Mama, I love him," she said, her voice strangled. "Please save him."

"You do?" Gracie whispered in disbelief.

"Aye."

Her mother arched an eyebrow at her, then whispered, "Good."

"Good?" Ashlyn was totally confused. She could see naught that was good in their desperate situation.

"Aye, 'tis about time you lost your heart to someone. Magnus will guard your heart well, once he awakens."

"Then…then you think he will?"

"Aye. He's a strong man, and if he knows how you feel, he will awaken for you. Now that the bandage is finished, why do you not go answer our laird's questions? Gracie can finish here with me. You can answer *my* questions later." Her mother winked and smiled as she rinsed out some linen squares to use on the wound.

Ashlyn moved into the other chamber where her uncles, Logan and Alex, sat with Jake and her stepsire. Jake stood and ushered her to a chair. "Come and sit. You look exhausted. If you've the strength, please tell us what transpired."

She explained about the cottage they'd used for shelter in the storm, and how they had found the dead deer and followed the tracks to the castle. Only two eyebrows quirked at the mention of the two of them staying alone in the hut—her stepsire's and Jake's. Naught was said by anyone. She gave them the general location of the new path, and how they had followed it to the crumbling keep.

"Logan tells me you believe 'twas MacNiven. Are you sure?"

"I saw him from afar with his helm on, but Magnus recognized him. The talk we overheard certainly sounded like him."

"Any idea what their plans are?" Uncle Alex asked, drumming his fingers on the table.

"When my arrows killed two of his men, MacNiven raced for the front of the keep. He gave instructions for one of the men to kill Magnus, then he whirled around and fled. The others followed him. I put an arrow in the belly of the man aiming for Magnus, and I tried to shoot MacNiven," she paused, trying to collect herself. "I caught him in the shoulder, but then I noticed Magnus was barely moving and another ran after him, so I shot him in his chest and climbed out of the tree."

The floodgates finally opened, and down came the tears. "I could have tried to shoot MacNiven again, but Magnus…I decided…the other man could have killed him." Her face now covered with tears, she was unable to finish her sentence.

Jake, seated next to her, wrapped his arm around her shoulder and kissed her cheek. "I'm quite pleased you chose to take care of my best friend instead of taking off after that fool. 'Twas the right thing to do."

"I could have put an end to all of this, but then I…"

"I would have done the same. I agree with Jake, you made the correct choice." Uncle Logan crossed his arms in front of his chest.

"We all agree, now you need to accept 'tis true." Uncle Alex stood and moved to the door, filling up the entire frame. "Jake, there's little more we can do. He's a strong warrior. I expect we'll talk to him by the morrow. Logan, come back to the great hall for an ale?"

Before they left, Alex stopped with his hand on the door handle. "Ashlyn, you alone wounded the man who has escaped all of us, you've made me proud to call you a Grant warrior. Hold your head high."

"My thanks, my laird." She sniffled because her tears had

finally slowed. The reality of what her laird had just said settled on her. Was it the truth? Was she the only warrior to have injured MacNiven? She fought with everything she had back at that curtain wall, but she'd been ready to go home when in Edinburgh. There was no reason to be embarrassed. Suddenly, she looked at all that transpired in a different light. Uncle Alex was proud of her!

Once they left, she dragged herself back into Magnus's room. Her mother had finished covering his wound with fresh linens. "Ashlyn, I'm finished. We'll let him sleep and hope he awakens in the morn. I'll stay the night with him. Why do you not go home with Gracie? You are exhausted."

"Nay, Mama. I'll stay. In fact, I'm going to climb into bed next to him. Why do you not go home and rest? Someone else may need you. I can care for him. I know this may not suit your sensibilities, but we have been traveling alone since Edinburgh."

Her mother stopped in her tracks to gaze at her daughter.

"I have verra few nightmares when he sleeps near me. 'Tis where I sleep best. In fact, he helped me to remember some of my past. I'll share with you another day." She climbed into his bed, cuddled next to him with her clothes on, and closed her eyes. "I'm tired, Mama."

She didn't see her mother leave with a smile on her face.

His eyes felt like they'd been sewn shut, but he managed to slowly peel them open. He was in a bed, in the middle of the night, judging by the darkness…but the last thing he recalled was heading home with Ashlyn after seeing MacNiven. Something warm lay beside him, and he smiled when her sweet scent reached him. He could think of no better way to awaken than with his Ashlyn tucked against him.

He kissed her forehead and she moved her head, her eyes opening, trying to focus.

"You are awake? Magnus, you are better?" She sat up enough to get a good look at him.

"Aye, lass. This is the way I wish to always awaken. But my memory fails me. How did we get here? The last thing I recall was trying to stay upright on my horse."

She filled Magnus in on the details, and his hands began to wander while she talked, caressing her hips, pulling at the ribbons on her gown.

"You must get yourself out of these garments. Get those trews off. If I'm to hold you, I wish to feel your soft skin, not rough wool."

She continued to talk while he helped her remove her clothing, then he nuzzled her neck before he stopped her story completely by melding his lips to hers. He delved deep into her mouth with his tongue, and she moaned—a beautiful sound. Then she broke the kiss and pulled back. Looking into his eyes, she said, "I love you, Magnus. I do not know if you remember me telling you."

"Aye, I do, and sweeter words I've never heard. You may say it as many times as you wish." His hands came up to cup her breasts, his thumbs rotating on top of her nipples.

"How is your leg? Does it pain you much?"

"Not a bit. Why? Is there something wrong with it?" He waggled his brow at her to let her know that something as inconsequential as a leg wound would not stop him in his pursuit of seeing her enjoy her sensuality again.

She lifted the sheet to peer at his bandage, then pulled his hands away with a sparkle in her eyes. "First, I shall check your bandage. And since I am caring for you, your instructions are to stay still and not overwork yourself." After checking his thigh—the bleeding had stopped, she told him—she turned her attention to something else that stood proudly at the juncture of his thighs. It was his natural reaction to her, and he could do little to stop it.

"Roll flat onto your back so I may inspect it closer."

He moved as instructed, believing she spoke of his injury. Then it dawned on him that she was speaking of his hardness, not his wound. He clasped his hands behind his head and grinned.

Moments later, he felt her tongue touch the tip of his cock, and he jerked in response. While he had guessed she was interested in playing a bit, he had expected the soft touch of her hand, not this.

"Ashlyn?" He lifted his head to stare at her.

"Silence. I must tend your needs," she said, her voice playful. She ran her tongue down the length of him and earned a moan in response to her teasing. Then she took him full in her mouth and sucked him, as he had done to her.

"Ashlyn, you need not..." A groan came from him unbidden, and he closed his eyes, deciding to surrender to her ministrations.

She continued with her sweet torture, licking and laving him until he could take it no more. "Up here."

She giggled. "You did not like what I was doing?"

"Aye, I did. But I wish for you to climax with me. You remember the hut?"

She wiggled in response at the memory of their time together. "Aye," she whispered. "I recall quite well, but I must be careful of your injury." She settled her hands on his chest and straddled him. After rubbing and teasing her entrance with his cock, she reached down to guide him inside of her. Her moan of delight set his pride to soaring, but he said naught, just smiled.

Moving up and down on him, she flicked his nipples with her nails, her response to him building, forcing her to move faster. He could see it in the line of her jaw. Reaching one hand down to caress her nub, he moved the other to her bottom.

Before long, she was shouting his name, milking her climax for what she could. When he knew she had finished, he moved his hands down to her hips and held her exactly where he wanted her most, so he could feel her contractions just so. She moved with him, and he grunted, finishing with a smile.

Ashlyn was a sweet pleasure indeed.

When she cuddled up to him, he had to ask her the question that had been on the tip of his tongue since he'd awakened. "I know we talked of other things, but I have changed. You have changed me." He kissed her forehead. "I no longer fear living my life to the fullest. Will you do me the honor of becoming my wife? I know I did not do this proper the other day, and you deserve better. I'm not good with words, but I know what is in my heart. Mayhap it is because I came close to losing my life, but I do not wish to wait. I want you more than aught. Marry me, Ash. I love you and I want you in my arms every day and every night."

He waited a moment for his question to settle in. It was probably a shock to her, but he meant every word. He ran his finger from her forehead down to her jawline. "I want you by my side forever."

She said naught, so he added, "If you need to think on it, 'tis all right. We've been through an ordeal, and we are both exhausted. Think on it for a couple of days and return to give me your answer."

"I…I'm sorry, Magnus. I do not wish to hurt you, but I would like to think on it. I love you, too, but so much has happened… I just need a wee bit of time." She gazed into his eyes and said, "I promise to give you an answer soon."

Disappointed but not surprised, he tugged her back down next to him. "Take all the time you need. I will be here waiting for you."

# CHAPTER EIGHTEEN

Ashlyn climbed up the hill back to her house just before dawn in the morning. She needed to clean up and change her clothes.

And think.

What was she to do? He had survived, thank the Lord, and she loved him, but was she ready to marry? Her mind twisted and turned in every possible direction, but she could not come up with a solution. She'd talk to her mother first, though she was quite sure she knew what her mama would say. Her mother would love to see her married.

But could a lass who had spent most of her life hating lads—or, at least, many lads—truly give herself to one? She entered the cottage, then closed the door quietly behind her in case anyone was still abed.

On the other hand, this was her chance. This was what she'd dreamed of for years. She could have it all—a man to love, bairns of her own. But would it be fair to saddle Magnus with a lass who still had nightmares? So far, their lovemaking had been wonderful, but would her past come back to haunt her? Aye, Magnus had helped settle the one nightmare, but the other? She'd had no luck retrieving any memories of two men.

There was also still the fear that she could not measure up to his previous wife. Would she be enough for him, or would he regret marrying her someday, wishing for Rhona instead? Would he abandon her in favor of a memory? Her heart was torn in two.

Her mother sat near the hearth, her usual morning spot, with her bowl of porridge.

"Are you the only one up, Mama?"

"Gracie is still asleep, and the lads slept with the guards last night. Robbie just left. How is Magnus?"

She sat in a chair by the fire, across from her mother. "He is better. He awoke about an hour or so ago, and I checked his dressing. There is just a wee bit of blood."

"Does he have a fever?"

"Nay, will he get one?"

"Aye, 'tis possible since the wound was not properly cleaned right away. If so, Magnus is strong—he should be able to fight the fever."

"I hope so." She stared into the dancing flames, wondering how to broach the subject of marriage with her mother.

"When is the wedding?" her mother whispered.

She spun her head around to stare at her. "What?"

"I asked when the wedding was going to take place."

"I do not understand why you would ask me such a question." She squirmed in her chair, suddenly feeling more exhausted than she had in days.

"Because I know he took your maidenhead."

"Mama, how could you know that?" She hated to lie to her mother, but she wasn't ready to be forced into marriage.

"I know my own daughter. Do you truly wish to play this game?"

Her shoulders slumped. "Nay."

Her mother cleared her throat. "Allow me to try a different tactic. Magnus took your maidenhead, did he not?"

All of a sudden, Ashlyn's temper flared. "Nay, he did not. I *gave* him my maidenhead. 'Twas a gift from me to him with no expectations." How she wished to leave and go to her bed chamber, but she needed to talk to her mother about marriage. Would this not be the perfect time?

"If I know Magnus, and I think I do, he has asked you to marry him. He may not have had the chance to speak with your stepsire because of his injury, but I am sure he discussed it with you."

Ashlyn was too weary to argue. She might as well confess all to her mother, she was no young lass but a woman. "Aye, he has offered. I know he would make a good husband, but I know not if 'tis what I want." She gave her mother a pleading look, hoping she would not attack her.

"Forgive me for mentioning this, but have you considered the possibility that you may be carrying his bairn?" Her mother carried her bowl over to the basin to wash it, not looking at her.

Ashlyn did not speak for a moment. It was foolish of her, but she had not considered that this possibility could happen to her. She had chosen to ignore the truth of the matter, but now she could not. How did one know? Her hand flew to her belly as if a mere touch would tell her.

"How would I know?" she whispered.

"If you did not get your courses as usual. Some women get nauseous in the morning, others do not. But I wish to warn you that the more often you lay with him, the better the chances that you will carry. And as of yet, there is no known way to prevent it, though some herbalists speak of certain tea mixtures and other such things. Naught is used with confidence." She returned to the chair by the hearth. "I hope you will agree to marry him if you are carrying his bairn. 'Twould be the right thing to do. 'Tis his bairn as well."

Ashlyn's mind was doing somersaults, but there could only be one answer. "Aye, if I am carrying. I will marry him."

"Ash, if you do not want a loving husband, what do you want? I know you have spent much of your life hating men, and I'm sure it's due to the life we led before moving to the Highlands. But our life is much better now. Surely, living here with the Grants and the Ramsays, seeing the happiness and the devotion shared by all these couples, can you not see that marriage might make you happy? I know you wished to stop MacNiven, and you should be verra proud of yourself for wounding him, but that does not mean you should not have a life of your own."

"Mama, I do not know what I want. I thought I would love traveling to Edinburgh, but I could not wait to come home. Magnus and I even came back early because I could not handle being away. While I was gone, I ended up in situations that frightened me so much that I was nauseous. 'Twas only by chance that we came upon MacNiven when we did."

"So you did not enjoy traveling with the guards as much as you thought you would?"

"Aye. I would not wish to be Aunt Gwyneth and travel freely. I like my clan. I missed all of you and Gracie." She fought to hold back her tears. "But...but I want to help. I need to help. Those women, Mama, they are still basically his prisoners. They do not know what he plans for them. I overheard them talking. They deserve to be free as any woman does."

"Aye, they do, but you are not the only one who can stop him. And loving someone does not mean you cannot continue to assist when possible. Can you not see how much Uncle Logan and Aunt Gwyneth love each other? They fight for justice, yet they have a family of their own, including adopted daughters. Ashlyn, inside you are angry and hurt, but you also have the biggest, most generous heart I've ever known. You mustn't think that you need to give up your own happiness to help other lasses."

"You're right, Mama. I'm verra tired. Would you mind if I went to bed? I know I have much to think on, and I promise I will. Magnus told me to take all the time I need, but I'd like to give him my answer within two days." She rubbed her forehead and stood.

Her mother wrapped her arms around her. "Ashlyn, I will help you in any way possible. Get some rest now. Your thinking will be clearer when you are well-rested."

"My thanks, Mama." She kissed her mother's cheek and headed to her bedroom.

As soon as she closed the chamber door behind her, she saw Gracie sitting up in bed, tears running down her cheeks. "Gracie, what's wrong?"

"I heard you talking to Mama. You're getting married?"

Ashlyn sat on the bed facing Gracie. How she adored her sister. They'd been sleeping in a big bed together forever. "I'm not sure. Why are you crying?"

"Because you're leaving me. We've always been together. I do not recall a time when you were not with me. What will I do without you?" Gracie swiped at the tears on her face.

"Gracie, I have not decided for sure yet. Magnus has asked me, but I have not accepted. Do you not wish to marry someday?" Ashlyn reached for the near white locks of her sister's hair, tucking some of the wild strands behind her ear. Gracie had hypnotizing blue eyes and the most beautiful skin Ashlyn had ever seen. Most knew from a glance that they were half-sisters, since their coloring was so different. Neither of them had ever met Gracie's sire, and their mother never spoke of him.

"Nay, I have not thought on it much. Mama keeps me busy."

"But with the way you love the wee ones, you would be a natural mother." Gracie was probably the most beautiful lass in all of the clan, but she had few suitors because her stepsire was the laird's brother, she stayed at home much of the time, and most were afraid of her beauty. "And you have a heart of gold."

Gracie stared at her hands as she twisted the linens back and forth on her lap. "No lads are interested in me. 'Tis as if they do not see me. I had always assumed you and I would grow old together."

"You are the most beautiful lass in the clan. The lads are *afraid* of you. Besides, you are so quiet you have not talked with many lads yet. You should go to the archery fields with me."

Her sister shook her head and scowled. "Nay, I'm not interested in lad's games. You may play them if you like, but they are not me." Her tears slowed as she looked into Ashlyn's eyes. "Do you think there is someone who would have me?"

"Gracie, there are many who would have you. Ask Robbie to find you a husband."

"Do you think Da would?" The hope in her sister's eyes saddened her.

Since Gracie had never known her sire, she had always referred to Robbie Grant as her da, but Ashlyn remembered hers, so she wished to respect her true sire by referring to Robbie as her stepsire. Robbie Grant, wonderful man that he was, did not mind either one. "I think it would make Da happy. Tell me the truth. Would you truly be so upset if I married? If so, mayhap I could ask Magnus if you could live with us."

"Nay. I shall stay here with Mama and Papa. Forgive my tears. I wish you happiness, Ashlyn. If you wish to marry Magnus, then you should do so. I'll be fine. 'Twas just such a surprise to me." She stared at her hands for a moment before lifting her gaze to Ashlyn's. "I do not mind if you marry, or even if you travel to Edinburgh, as long as you promise to never leave Grant land for good. I could not bear to lose you. Promise?"

Ashlyn felt as if she'd been hit by a thunderbolt. In her heart, she knew she could never leave either. "I would not be far, just down the hill. And mayhap someday you would be an aunt."

That made Gracie smile, her face now lit up with the thoughts of a bairn to love. "I would love to be an aunt."

Ashlyn gave her sister a hug. They settled onto the mattress and Ashlyn rolled on to her side. "Forgive me, Gracie, but I tire." She closed her eyes dreaming about a man with a permanent smile on his face.

It was mid-morning when she awakened with a scream. Hands were trying to grab her, and she tried to hit them and send them away. This was her other recurrent nightmare, the one with two men. It was a dream she hated even more than the other, mayhap because she did not recognize these men. Who knew if they were out there still?

Gracie came in and wrapped an arm around her shoulders, assisting her to a sitting position. "Another nightmare? 'Twas the same as the others?"

"Aye, 'tis the dream with two men. The ones I do not recognize."

Gracie hugged her and kissed her cheek. "I feel terrible that you continue to experience these dreams."

"Do you know I have had fewer nightmares when Magnus was near? The first time was when we were in Edinburgh and he had to sleep outside the door. Then I had another one. The only other time he held me while I cried. 'Twas nice."

"But only two in all that time? You were gone a fortnight. That is an improvement."

"Gracie, may I ask you a question?"

Gracie sat back so she could look into her sister's eyes and nodded. "Of course. You know I would do aught for you."

"Do you recall aught about the time before we came to live here? When the Norse came, or when we traveled through the Highlands with Uncle Logan and Aunt Gwyneth? I know you were young, around two summers, but surely you must recall something."

"Nay, I have tried many times, but I have no memories at all from that time."

"Mama thinks if I could remember the dreams and talk about them, the nightmares would cease. I can recall one, but not the other. It feels wrong to marry someone when I am riddled with nightmares."

Her mother entered their chamber. "Another one, Ashlyn?"

"Aye. The one with the two men."

"Mama, Ashlyn tells me that she does not have as many nightmares when Magnus is near," Gracie said, looking at their mother.

"That makes sense to me. He is her protector, and in case you think you do not need one, Ashlyn, think of Aunt Gwyneth. She is a highly capable lass, but she goes nowhere without Uncle Logan."

"Aye. 'Tis true, I know," Ashlyn said, rubbing her head. "Have you been to see Magnus yet?"

"Aye, he is much better. I stitched his wound this morn because it broke open again. I could see better in the light of day. He is a tough man. I changed the linen strips and brought him some broth. He is still weak, but he shall survive."

"I think I shall go see him after I wash up and change into a clean gown."

"May I go with you this time?" Gracie asked. "Since you are in love with him, I would like to get to know him better." She grinned at her sister. "He must be quite special to have caught your eye."

"Aye, I'll be ready to go in a wee bit." She moved into the other room but then stopped to speak to Gracie. "Aye, he is quite special. You'll see."

"Daughter, you must eat something. You lost weight on this journey, and you look thin now. When was the last time you ate?" Her mother stared at her, assessing her from head to toe.

She thought for a moment and realized she hadn't eaten since the previous morning. Aunt Gwyneth had given her an oatcake while they rode toward Clan Grant, but that was all she could recall. "Aye, Gracie, would you make me a bowl of porridge please?"

Gracie left and her mother squeezed her. "I think you must realize how telling it is that you haven't had many nightmares around Magnus. This tells me two things. You trust him, and he is good for you."

"Aye." Her mother left, so she stripped down and finished her ablutions. While she had hoped that the night would somehow answer her most pressing question, her head only felt more muddled.

She knew one thing for sure: she already missed him.

Soon she was sitting at the table, eating the porridge her sister had prepared for her. Gracie sat across from her and whispered,

"Have you decided yet?"

Ashlyn's mother, fussing around the chamber, said nary a word, but it was obvious she had overheard the question.

"Nay," Ashlyn insisted. "'Tis a most important decision, one that should not be made in a matter of moments." Slud, how she lied. She wished a wee fairy had come to her in the middle of the night and told her what to do. She hated making decisions when she was uncertain.

An hour later, she and Gracie headed down the hill toward Magnus's house. When they were almost there, she noticed two lads approaching the hut with a pair of Deerhounds. She guessed them to be Magnus's dogs. The lads knocked on the door just before Gracie and Ashlyn arrived, and the Deerhounds each barked once and sniffed the sisters while they ran around them in circles. When the door opened, both dogs went straight for their master, yelping and squealing and running in a frenzy, clearly excited to see their master again. One of them was so excited that he bucked like a wild horse trying to escape training.

Magnus limped over to a stool at his table, laughing and talking to his pets while he soothed them.

"Mada, did you have fun with the lads' dogs? Were you a good lad, Sim?" The two jumped and pranced around Magnus, stopping only occasionally to take a sniff of his wound under the bandage. When they finally calmed, Magnus instructed them to sit, so they sat, panting, and then actually lay at his feet.

Ashlyn stuck her head through the open door and giggled. "I do not think they will be leaving you anytime soon, Magnus."

She knew him well enough to know the smile he gave her was false this time. Fear gathered in her belly. Something was wrong.

Magnus thanked the lads for caring for his dogs and they left, pleased with the small daggers he had found for them in Edinburgh.

"Have you had aught to eat this morn?" Gracie asked him as she and Ashlyn walked into the living area of his hut.

Magnus stared at the beams in his ceiling with a baffled expression on his face. "I'm not certain. I must have because my stomach is not growling. I do not feel hungry at all."

He looked from Ashlyn to Gracie and back again, but his eyes were glazed over. She could see the sweat beaded on his forehead, so she leaned over and touched her cheek to his forehead. The fear in her belly swelled. "Magnus, you're burning up. You have the fever."

Magnus sighed. "I know. I suspected as much. I do not feel well, and all I wish to do is sleep. I tried to stay up until I saw you and the dogs, but now I'd like to go to my bed and sleep."

Ashlyn turned to face her sister. "Gracie, will you go get Mama?" she asked, trying to keep her voice even. "I think she needs to see him. Tell her he has the fever. I think she may have something for it."

As soon as Gracie left the hut, her pace became more of a run than a walk. Ashlyn took Magnus's arm and helped him into bed. As soon as she tucked him in, he closed his eyes. A moment later, he opened them and said, "Rhona, is that you?"

# CHAPTER NINETEEN

"Nay, Magnus, 'tis me, Ashlyn." Tears misted her eyes, but she managed to keep them at bay.

"Rhona, I must talk to you. I plan to marry another. I'll miss you, but I love Ash. You'd love her, too. I hope you do not mind." He rolled onto his side and stared at the wall, as if he could see something Ashlyn could not. "But I wish for you to know that I will always have a special place in my heart for you. Ash holds a different place. You always said I was a big enough man to be two people. I find I love two. I have to wait for Ashlyn to decide, but she is worth the wait. I hope she says aye."

Ashlyn's heart almost burst out of her chest. She had her answer; she only hoped it was not too late. "Aye, Magnus. I'll marry you. I love you. We can marry and live here together. You just have to get better."

"Ash, is that you?" He glanced over his shoulder at her. "I'm verra tired. I love you. I hope you will be my wife. You are so beautiful and intelligent and brave. Did I tell you how proud I am of you? You, a lass, are the only one who did any damage to MacNiven. All the Ramsays and the Grants tried... Please say aye." His voice faded away as he drifted into slumber.

Ashlyn tucked him in again and the dogs came in and found a place at the foot of his bed.

He opened his eyes. "Ash, I'm cold."

He shivered, so she glanced around for another plaid and found one in a chest against the wall. She yanked it out and dragged it over to the bed, but when she unfurled it over the mattress, a night rail fell on the floor at her feet. Once she covered him, she picked up the white night gown and held it up next to her.

"Lass, 'tis Rhona's. She was just a wee thing; you'll never fit into her clothes. I should throw them away."

"Aye, I can see I am a wee bit larger than she was." She returned the small item to the chest.

His chuckle made her scowl, but then he said, "I will not have to worry about whether I hurt you when I make love to you. We shall have a wild time together." He snorted and his breathing changed.

Everything he'd said was true. They would have a wild time together in bed, and she did not mind that she was larger than Rhona. She never would have survived all she had endured if she'd been petite.

She'd agreed to marry him, but her words did not seem to have registered in his mind. Mayhap he was too sickly. She would tell him again as soon as he awakened.

She leaned over to place a chaste kiss on his forehead. "You must fight this first, Magnus. Please do it for me. When you wake up, we will marry, and we will be ever so happy."

A few moments later, Ashlyn's mother rushed into the bed chamber. "How bad is his fever? Was he still able to talk?"

"Aye, but he was not making sense. He thought I was Rhona."

"Och, they get delirious sometimes. You cannot trust what they tell you when they are delirious. Do not worry." Her mother pulled a few items out of her satchel and set them on the chest.

"He did not say aught that I did not like. He really loves me, Mama. I do wish to marry him." The last sentence ended with a sob.

Her mother handed a container to her. "Help me put these herbs on his chest, and see if we can get him to drink this. It may make his fever pass more quickly."

Ashlyn did her best to awaken Magnus while her mother left the chamber to gather the rest of her things. When she returned, Ashlyn took Magnus's hand in hers and rubbed the skin on the back. "Wake up just for a moment. We need you to drink this, Magnus. 'Twill help with the fever."

After much pushing and prodding, Magnus finally lifted his head with Ashlyn's assistance. As soon as his gaze fell on her, a huge smile crossed his face. "Good morn, love."

"Drink this for me, please?"

"I'd do aught for you, you know that."

Her mother winked at her and held the goblet to his lips. To Ashlyn's relief, he managed to get most of it down before his head fell back against the pillow.

Once they finished treating him, they moved back into the main chamber to let him get some rest. "Gracie did not return with me. Your aunt Madeline wished to speak with her, so she went to the keep." She paused, then said, "I was hoping we could talk a little about your nightmares, Ashlyn. No matter what you say, I cannot help but feel at fault for them. I did everything I could to protect you and Gracie, but mayhap 'twas not enough. I believe something happened to you that I knew naught about. Mayhap something involving Malcolm, or some other man who came to my house."

"Mama, this is not necessary. I do not fault you. In fact, I know one of the instances, I just did not wish to tell you about it."

"Please, for me? This troubles me as much as it troubles you. If you are to marry and start a new life, 'tis important for you to be settled with the past."

She finally nodded, and her mama led her over to the table. "Please tell me about the one incident that you recall," Ashlyn's mother said. "I need to know. My heart needs to know. What did I miss?"

She could see the tears her mother was trying to hold back, and she debated whether or not to tell her, but ultimately it was the right thing to do. Just before she started her story, Aunt Gwyneth entered the hut.

"How is he?" She came in and hung her mantle on the wall.

"He has a fever, but his wound looks fine," Ashlyn's mother said. "Come and sit with us. Mayhap you can help us."

Gwyneth frowned. "What is it? I'll try if I can, but you two look verra serious."

"Ashlyn has had nightmares ever since we came to Clan Grant. She had another one last night. My hope is that if we can help her remember the source, they will no longer trouble her."

"The same kind of nightmare you had in Edinburgh, Ashlyn?" Gwyneth sat down at the table with them.

"Aye, but that one concerned the man who had abducted me that night."

"Och, Ashlyn. You have not told me much about that."

Ashlyn's mother glanced at Aunt Gwyneth, but fortunately, her aunt did not reply.

"That discussion can wait, Mama." She took a deep breath, then continued. "I've had two kinds of nightmares, one in which one man is trying to touch me and Gracie, and another in which there are two men. I recall the incident that led to the first one, but not the second one. 'Tis the dream that awakened me last night. I've had it for years." She brushed her hair out of her eyes in frustration. She'd done naught to tame her unruly tresses today. In a short time, she'd truly come to rely on Magnus.

Caralyn nodded her head. "We're listening. Go ahead. I'll do my best not to interrupt."

While she talked, Aunt Gwyneth got up and stood behind her, combing her hair with her fingers and plaiting it. "The incident I recall happened the night after the Norse attacked."

"When you hid near the beach," her mama said. She was gripping the edge of the table with white knuckles.

"Aye. We did as you said. I thought we'd never see you again, so I found a place for us to sleep in the trees. I woke up when a man was touching me, so I hit him and he ran away." She decided that was all she needed to tell her mother. She left out the part about Gracie and about how she'd stabbed the fool.

"So that is the source of one of your dreams?"

"Aye. I'm certain of that, and all my memories of that night have returned. He attempted to defile us, but he did not. He ran away, and I never saw him again." She realized now that he had likely escaped—though she'd spent years thinking she'd caused the man's death, Magnus had helped her see the more likely truth. "But this other dream, I only remember bits and pieces of it. I know not when it happened."

"Tell us more," Aunt Gwyneth said.

"There are two men. One reaches for me and I hit him, and then he tries to touch Gracie and I hit him. That is all that returns to me. I wake up screaming trying to hit him."

"And the man does not look like Malcolm?" her mama pressed.

"Nay. Nor does he look like any other of your acquaintances. I remember them, and I recall how much you warned them all about touching us. In fact, Mama, now I understand everything you did and why you did it." She looked into her eyes as she said it, needing her mama to know how much she appreciated all she'd done for them.

"Go on," Aunt Gwyneth said. "I want to hear more about the two men."

"One is big and the other is thin. They are both dirty and reek terribly. The thin one tries to touch us, and I hit him, and the big one always says the same thing. 'Leave them be. They are too young, Fingal.' I recall that from last night's dream. I know no one named Fingal. Do you recall someone named Fingal, Mama?"

Her mother shook her head. "Nay. I never met a man named Fingal."

"I do," Gwyneth said, staring at her with an intent expression. "I know who Fingal is." She finished plaiting Ashlyn's hair before moving to the seat across from her. "I know exactly where that is from. Your mother was never there, but I was."

Ashlyn glanced at her mother, but there was no recognition in her mother's glance. Then her mother gasped and said, "Do you think so, Gwyneth? From near the creek with Robbie and Logan?"

"Aye. 'Twas when your uncle and I found you," Gwyneth said, reaching out to take her hand. "Malcolm sent you away with two fool men so he could control your mother. 'Twas right after I met Logan."

Caralyn's face fell into her hands. Gwyneth continued. "You were held in a shabby hut by two men who were brothers. We searched almost all of the burgh before we found you. I doubt you were fed much because you were thin as can be, and I recall that you smelled almost as much as they did."

Ashlyn looked aghast. "I do not recall aught about it."

"Probably not. Your mind must have blocked the memory. Sometimes the mind does what it must to protect us. Do you know one of the reasons you were so upset?"

A tear trickled down her cheek as just the faintest of memories came back to her. Her aunt had given her a clue, something that had jarred her memory. She and Gracie had smelled. Her hand moved to her nose, rubbing it as the memory returned.

Aunt Gwyneth reached for her hand. "You were upset because you smelled. You hadn't bathed in weeks, and Gracie was still in rags. You told me you were only allowed to change her rag once a day. Robbie, Tomas, Uncle Logan, and I found you, and we had to kill the two louts in front of you, which was not a pleasant experience. That could be why you pushed it out of your memory. At your age, that must have been traumatic for you.

"But the first thing you said after the fools were no longer a threat was that you were dirty." She laughed. "And I was so young I had no idea what to do with you. 'Twas your uncle Logan who stepped up. Robbie wanted to take you away from there as you were, but Uncle Logan said nay because he had taken care of Lily and Torrian when they had been sick. He knew how important cleanliness was to young ones. He ordered all of us to carry water up from the creek."

Caralyn had tears running down her face when she lifted her face from her hands. "Do you remember?" she asked, staring into her eyes.

"I do. 'Tis coming back in bits and pieces. Did Uncle Logan take Gracie's rag off and dip her bottom in a basin, making her laugh?"

"Aye." Aunt Gwyneth smiled at her.

"Ashlyn, I'm confused," Ashlyn's mother said. "I have asked you before if those two men were the ones in your nightmares and you always said nay."

"Because I had no memories about it at all. I'm still not sure those are the two men, but the memory of that incident is returning to me." She glanced at Aunt Gwyneth for confirmation. "And Uncle Logan gave me a basin and held a plaid up so I could wash myself and no one could see me. He even had a sliver of soap. It smelled wonderful, fresh and sweet."

"All true. Now, can you remember the two? Fingal was thin, the other was taller and had a big belly…"

Ashlyn stood so fast that she knocked over the stool. She burst into tears. "Aye, 'twas them. He wanted to touch us and do other things." Her arms swung over her head as if the lout stood in front of her and she could pummel him with her fists. "Fingal did. He tried to touch us in the middle of the night—" her breath hitched, "—but the big one stopped him. Saints above, I recall."

"Good, tell me what else you remember." Her mother continued to push her.

"The place was so dirty." Her eyes snapped shut and her hands braced her head as if she could prevent the images from bombarding her mind. "It smelled, they smelled...*we* smelled." She wanted to bend over and retch, to put an end to the awful thoughts. She tugged on her plait as tears coursed down her face. "Gracie clung to me like never before. As wee as she was, it was as if she knew he was bad, bad to his core."

She opened her eyes and stared at Aunt Gwyneth, then at her mother. "I remember. They only gave us one oatcake a day, yet they would stuff their faces in front of us, smacking their lips and chuckling. Gracie was so hungry."

"And you gave your oatcake to Gracie, did you not?" Her mother swiped a tear of her own away.

"Aye. The first two days Gracie cried because she was hungry, but we both got used to it. And we went outside, and the rags were dirty. Mama, it was so vile." She threw herself at her mother, wrapping her arms around her.

"I'm so sorry, Ashlyn. I feel awful." Her mother held her tight, and Ashlyn let herself take comfort in her soothing, familiar scent.

"Mama, 'twas not your fault."

"Aye, 'twas all my fault. Malcolm did this to you..."

"Stop it, Mama." She stepped back to stare at her mother. "Stop. I want you to never say those awful words again. 'Twas not your fault. Now I understand. I know what you did for us. You gave yourself to a man so Gracie and I could eat. I remember Malcolm coming in with the bag of carrots and turnips, and how he would refuse to feed us until you agreed to give him what he wanted. The way he teased us was so loathsome. How could you blame yourself for giving in to him?"

Tears covered her mother's face. "I could not bear to see either of you hungry."

"I know what you did for us. Oh, Mama." She wrapped her arms around her mother as she sobbed on her shoulder. "You gave up your dignity for us, Mama."

"He was not as bad as you think, not in the beginning."

Ashlyn nodded and pulled away from her mother to look at her aunt. "And you, dear Auntie, I recall now. You came in and one of the bad men put a knife to your throat. 'Twas you and Robbie who motioned for us to be quiet in the corner. And Uncle Logan came in through the back door. They were going to kill us and you, but Uncle Logan stopped them, because he said you belonged to him."

Aunt Gwyneth, too choked up to speak, said, "Aye. 'Tis true. He did not mention you two because he was trying to draw attention away from you. I hated your uncle then."

"Why? How could you hate Uncle Logan? He rescued you, and he saved us from those horrid men." She could hardly believe what her aunt had said, but she recalled they argued often on the journey up to the Highlands.

"I hated him and everything he represented for the same reasons you once hated men, lass. Because they had hurt me so much. But there are many good men, and I think you know that now as much as I do. I love your uncle and marrying him was the best decision I ever made. You can still help other women if you marry."

"Auntie, Magnus has asked me to marry him. I love him. Would you think less of me if I married and wished to stay here? I did not like traveling to Edinburgh."

"Nay. You are a mighty brave lass. You have protected your sister ever since you were eight. You have naught to be ashamed of. Marry Magnus if that is what's in your heart. You will be wonderful together. He is a good man."

Ashlyn hugged her aunt and her mother. "I love you, Aunt Gwyneth, Mama. Mama, would you mind if I went to see Gracie? She should know that I've finally remembered."

Her mother and Gwyneth both hugged her again, and she took several steps toward the door. "Wait one moment." She ran back into the bed chamber and kissed Magnus, who was still fast asleep. When she reached the front the door, she stopped and turned to her mother. "Mama, promise me something?"

"Aye?"

"Promise me you'll never again say 'twas your fault?"

Her mother clasped her hands in front of her and nodded. "Go see your sister."

# CHAPTER TWENTY

Ashlyn tore across the field, running up the hill without slowing. She flew into her cottage and yelled out, "Gracie?"

Gracie emerged from their bed chamber. "What is it? And before I forget, Uncle Logan wishes to see you at the keep, but I'll tell you my news before you go."

Ashlyn felt her heart swell as she stared at her sister. It amazed her that Gracie could think no one would ever be interested in her. She was so beautiful and so pure of heart. She rushed over and grasped Gracie's hands in hers. "I've remembered it all. Every bit of what was causing my nightmares. It came back when I started to talk to Mama and Aunt Gwyneth."

"Wonderful! Or at least it will be if it will help prevent any further nightmares. Go ahead and tell me all about it." She smiled and waited for Ashlyn to continue.

Ashlyn thought for a moment before deciding there was no reason to tell her sister about that horrible time in their lives. Perhaps it would be best if Gracie never knew. "If you do not mind, I would rather not talk about it again. 'Twould be best if I never thought of the incident again. Would that be agreeable to you?"

"Aye. I do not need to know. May I tell you my news?" Her eyes shone bright with excitement.

"Of course," Ashlyn said, curious about what had excited her sister.

"Come sit with me."

"Go ahead. I cannot wait to hear what you have to tell me."

"I hope you will not be upset with me. I do not know what decision you have made about Magnus, but Aunt Maddie approached me at the keep. She asked me if I would be willing to teach the wee lassies who were rescued from Castle Dubh— Maeve, Morna, and Maisie. In fact, she asked me if I would sleep in the same room as them. She'd also like me to play with them and take them for walks. We're to have our own chamber. 'Tis quite a large one she has chosen with a short table and stools she had built for the wee ones. But you know how important reading is to Aunt Maddie."

"And did you agree to it?"

"I did. I'm quite excited. You know how I love the wee ones, and this way I will meet more people in the keep. All the guards eat there a few nights a week. Mayhap I will meet someone. Plus, Aunt Maddie said Aline would take over for me one day a week so I could come home and spend the day with you and Mama and Da."

Ashlyn got up and tugged her sister out of the chair. "Gracie, I think this is a wonderful idea. I'm so happy for you."

"You are not upset? I did not know if you were planning to stay here or marry Magnus."

"Nay, I am not upset. This will be wonderful for you. And I think I will marry Magnus, though I'm still thinking on it." Ashlyn believed it was just what Gracie needed to meet more people. "Have you talked to Mama yet?"

"Nay, but I think she'll be agreeable. Aunt Maddie said she plans to ask Cook to teach us all how to make a few things. She promised the lassies they could learn how to make sweet pastries."

"Aye, I think Mama will be quite pleased." Ashlyn loved the glow radiating from her sister's face.

"Uncle Alex was there, too, and he said that while their hearts are big enough for the young ones, he's found their bones are not. Wee Maeve is verra busy, and Maddie cannot keep up with her without exhausting herself. I was thinking of some games we can play in the snow. Forgive me. I need not blather on so. I shall return to my packing. Do not forget to go visit with Uncle Logan. He wanted to see you within an hour."

"I'll go now." She grabbed her mantle and hurried out on her horse. She had no idea what Uncle Logan could want, especially since Aunt Gwyneth had not mentioned aught about it.

Riding in the wind made her realize how much better she felt.

There were no niggling fears in the back of her mind, no questions about who had tried to attack her, or who could be returning to find her. Those two men from the hut were dead; they would never bother her or Gracie again.

Her decision was made, and she felt quite confident about it, she just didn't wish to share it with anyone until she talked to Magnus. She loved him, and she was beginning to believe she belonged by his side. If he would just get through this fever, they could discuss marriage. Listening to Aunt Gwyneth speak about Uncle Logan had opened her eyes.

The stable lad helped her dismount and then stabled her horse. She tore up to the great hall, anxious to see what her uncle wanted. Mayhap MacNiven had been caught, though it was a little too early for a messenger to have arrived.

She knocked on the door to the solar, and Uncle Logan swung it open, a smile on his face.

"Ashlyn, so pleased to see you. Come in. Jake and your uncle Alex and I were just discussing you."

Ashlyn stepped inside. Uncle Alex, Uncle Logan, and Jake were the only three inside. It took her a moment to realize she was kneading her hands from nerves.

"How is Magnus this morn?" Jake asked. "I'll stop by later to check on him."

"He has a fever. Mama gave him some herbs and he's sleeping, though she thought his wound did not look any worse."

Uncle Logan nodded. "Good to hear that his wound should heal. He's a strong man. He'll beat the fever."

Ashlyn nodded and allowed Jake to usher her into a seat in front of Uncle Alex's desk. He gave her shoulder a quick squeeze before stepping back. She supposed her face was still a bit red from all the crying she had done with her mother.

Uncle Logan crossed his arms and leaned against Uncle Alex's desk. "I suppose you are wondering why we have requested your presence."

"Aye." She could think of naught else to say, so she just decided to wait for him to speak. She knew it was rare for a female other than the laird's wife to be called into the laird's solar. Granted, Aunt Gwyneth had been here many times.

"This is at the request of our king. He has given me strict

instructions to do everything in my power to catch MacNiven. You and Magnus have seen the bastard; you have wounded him. By the instructions of King Alexander, I am to request that you return to Edinburgh with me and assist in our quest to bring the man to justice. He cheated his hanging by paying someone to die for him—probably someone who had been sentenced to die anyway, and wanted coin for his family. Either way, our king means to see him hang."

Ashlyn could not believe what he had just asked her to do. She would be returning to Edinburgh?

"I know you have just returned to Clan Grant, and at your own request, Ashlyn, but you are the only one who was able to wound the man. The king has asked us to send out the team most likely to take down MacNiven. You are the obvious choice."

Uncle Alex said in a quiet voice. "Ashlyn, 'tis rare for a lass to be requested to represent the king on any type of mission. Your aunt is the only other female I know of who has been asked to serve the king in such a way."

For some reason, this was not settling in to her brain. What exactly were they asking her to do?

Uncle Logan said, "You could probably be put in charge of the group of guards sent to retrieve him if you are interested. In my opinion, you've earned it. Men like MacNiven are hard to kill. They know how to hide and they know how to make sure they are always protected. The fact that you wounded him earns you the right to lead. 'Tis your choice."

Ashlyn could not believe she had just been asked to lead a group of warriors in the search for Ranulf MacNiven, criminal and abuser of lasses.

Her dream job. Or at least it had been.

They were asking her to do what she'd always wished to do, this time for her king.

She was so stupefied, she could not think of the right words.

"Why do you not think about it before you give us an answer?" Jake said, clearly noticing her inner torment.

"Aye," Uncle Logan said. "Think on it, but we leave on the morrow, early in the morn. I'll need your answer by then."

She nodded, more confused than ever. "I'd like to speak with my parents, but I will return before this eve to give you my answer."

"Accepted."

They all stood. Before she left, Uncle Alex said, "Lass, it pleases me to tell you how proud I am, not just as your laird, but as your uncle. You found and injured our enemy when no one else could. Well done." He moved to her side and kissed her cheek.

She'd just received the one honor she'd always wanted. Her laird and Uncle Logan had congratulated her and were rewarding her for the job she'd done as a warrior. This was more than she'd ever thought possible. Her eyes misted, but she kept her tears at bay. Somehow she knew this to be a turning point in her life, a moment she would always remember, always cherish. She'd done it. She'd not only performed as a man, she'd *outperformed* many men. What more could she ask for? She had to go, did she not?

But her heart was not leaping with joy, and the main reason was someone with arms the size of tree trunks and a heart just as big.

Before she left, Ashlyn spun around to ask, "What about Magnus? He was with me."

"He would be invited if he were hale and hearty, but he is not," Uncle Logan replied. "At least not to leave on the morrow. We have not decided on the final team yet, but you are the only one presently at the Grant keep who has been asked to join. Jamie, Braden, Molly, Sorcha, Tormod, Coll, and Art may be asked to participate once we reach Edinburgh. I'll see what we discover when we arrive at the royal keep. If you decide to lead, you will have say on the rest of the team."

Ashlyn thanked them all and left. What the hell was she to do now?

# CHAPTER TWENTY-ONE

Ranulf MacNiven cursed again for the tenth time. He'd finally managed to get the arrow out of his shoulder, tip intact, but it hurt like the devil since he'd had to dig so deep. Those foolish Grants. Why in hell could they not just stay away?

How many times had a Grant or a Ramsay ruined everything for him? He'd planned so carefully each time. His first plot, which he'd hatched with Glenn and Dugald Buchan, had been for Davina to marry the new chieftain of the Ramsay clan. That would have been the easiest scheme, and it had almost taken place. He would have killed Torrian Ramsay and gained control of the Ramsay land in less than a year.

But a foolish wee lass had ruined his chances by revealing his plot before the king. He'd set it up to look like Torrian had deflowered Davina—an act that would have forced the marriage. The lassie had offered him *another* vial of chicken blood in front of the king, revealing all. Someone must have assisted her. She was too young to have planned it all so carefully and so well.

No matter. The fault lay at all the Ramsays' feet.

Then he'd had everything set in the Highlands. He'd kept his identity hidden, found a wealthy fool who was not very smart, and convinced him to finance his venture of taking over the Grants. If he had managed to take over the Grants, it would have been an easy matter to then attack the Ramsays. Failure again. This time because his foolish partner had relations with the lass belonging to the Grant heir. In so doing, he had brought Alexander Grant and over three hundred warriors down on them just to save his son.

Fool. Stupid fool, though he'd lost his life over his foolishness. Ranulf had been fortunate to get away with a few guards and no injuries…and a bagful of coins.

His next misfortune had been when he'd lost men in an apparent skirmish at the ravine, but he hadn't been there to see who was to blame for that travesty. He'd guess the Grants since they hadn't been far from their land. Bastards were everywhere.

After all of that, MacNiven and his men had been ambushed by a warrior wearing the Grant plaid while they were taking shelter from an unexpected storm. It seemed there was nowhere he could escape them.

He had to get to the Buchans, and naught would stop him, though some bastard had tried by putting an arrow in his shoulder.

He knew what he had to do. He'd make them all pay. He just had to decide the perfect attack. There was only one person who popped into his mind, but he'd have to give it more thought. This time he'd be careful, not haphazard as he'd been before. They would not stop him this time.

She left the great hall and wove through the courtyard, so absorbed in her thoughts she spoke to no one. The stable lad had her horse ready for her, so she mounted and headed back to her hut.

She decided to stop to see who was there. More than anything, she wished to talk with her mother, but she also hoped to find out what Aunt Gwyneth and Robbie thought of the offer she'd been given. Gracie was happy, so she wouldn't disturb her, and she could always count on Gracie's support.

Her stomach did a strange flop whenever she thought of the other implications if she were to accept this challenge.

She would have to leave Magnus—mayhap for a long time. Uncle Logan and Uncle Alex wanted to put their team together immediately, and she had to agree with them that time was not on their side. Even if his fever was gone by morn, Magnus would not be ready to fight. His wound was too fresh. But was she ready to leave the man she loved?

When she arrived at her cottage, she was surprised to see an extra horse there. She stepped inside and froze. All eyes were on her—her mother's, her stepsire's, Aunt Gwyneth's and Gracie's.

"Well?" her mother asked. "What did you decide?"

"You know?"

"Aunt Gwyneth told me after you left. Magnus awakened for long enough to eat something, and his fever was better, so we left Mada and Sim there as his protectors. He was going to try to sleep a bit more."

"I hope you know how proud we all are that you have been invited to do this," Robbie said. "Whether you choose to go or not, Uncle Logan will tell all the Ramsays and the Grants that you were the first choice to lead the group. He believes in you as much as he does in his own wife and his daughters."

"But I do not know what to do." She removed her mantle and stood in the middle of the hut as if she were lost.

Robbie said, "I understand your confusion, but is this not what you have always wanted? You will be fighting alongside the king's warriors."

"You have worked so hard at your archery," Caralyn added. "If 'tis what you want, you deserve this honor. You are as good or better than many of the men out there, but you know we will support you no matter what you decide." There was a knowing look in her eyes, but Ashlyn did not know what decision her mother thought she would—or should—make.

"How did you feel when you were in Edinburgh?" Aunt Gwyneth asked. "I know 'twas what you wished for more than aught, but 'twas not quite what you had thought 'twould be, was it?"

"Aye and nay, does that make sense? Aye, 'twas invigorating when we tracked the bastard and when I was able to put an arrow in his sorry hide. But there was much of it I did not like at all." She stared at the dear faces of her family. "I did not like being away from home. I cannot explain why." Her mother's face shone bright at this confession, but she continued, "Being attacked, being kidnapped…it frightened me more than anything has except for when…when…well, I think you know. Much of my past has returned, and I would prefer to put it all behind me and live for this day. Yet 'tis such an honor. Mayhap I could go this once." Ashlyn moved over to the fire to stare into the flames, rubbing her hands together to warm them. "I know not what to do."

No one said a word until Gracie came forward and gave her a hug. "Congratulations, sister. I knew you would prove your worth to everyone. Well done."

Ashlyn stared at her sister. "But I do not know what I should do."

Gracie took her sister's hand in hers and said, "I'm not verra experienced in life as the others are, but I think you should be asking yourself what you want to do, not what you think you *should* do. I accepted Aunt Maddie's offer because I love bairns. They make my heart sing. It was not because I believed everyone else thought I should do it. So what makes *your* heart sing?"

Ashlyn thought about what everyone had said, and suddenly, she knew she needed to speak to someone else before she made her final decision.

"Thank you, Gracie." She kissed her sister's cheek and grabbed her mantle. "Forgive me, but I must confer with someone else." Before she stepped through the door, she stopped and said, "I love you all so much, and I thank you. I promise to let you know my decision before I go talk with Uncle Logan this eve."

When she reached the bottom of the hill, she knocked on the door of the wee cottage. Mada and Sim barked, but she heard Magnus's bellowed greeting, so she stepped inside the hut.

He was still abed, but his coloring had improved.

"You are better, Magnus?"

"Aye." He sat up in bed, propping himself up with a pillow, and opened his arms toward her. "You have a difficult decision to make. Tell me about it."

She climbed into the bed, tucking herself next to him, her favorite place. "You heard about it?"

"Aye, I overheard your mother and your aunt discussing it. When do you leave?"

"On the morrow if I choose to go." She rested her head on his shoulder, wishing to memorize everything about this man to keep her warm at night on the journey.

"What do you mean if you choose to go? This is what you've always wanted, is it not? You must go. You've worked so hard at the archery field."

"Aye, 'tis all true, but I have mixed feelings."

"We are all proud of you. Why the mixed feelings? I hope 'tis not due to any concern over me. I am improving. And you need not answer my proposal until you return."

Ashlyn cupped his cheeks in her hands. "I must admit 'tis what I've always dreamed of, yet now it does not hold the same appeal without you. Am I a fool?"

She gave him a chaste kiss on the lips, but he changed it into a kiss that told her how much he cared about her. Would she risk losing him if she left for a moon or so, or worse yet, if the snow prevented her return until spring?

"You are not a fool, but I do not understand your hesitation."

She snuggled against him and took a deep sigh. "You know how much I respect my aunt Gwyneth and Molly and Sorcha. I respect all warriors, but the female warriors even more." She paused. This next bit was hard to say, but she had to come out with it. "And yet, now that I understand what warriors deal with every day, I must admit I am not as excited about it. I was so frightened when I was attacked… I do not ever wish to feel that way again."

"Your cousins would give their lives for you just as I would." His thumb brushed across the sensitive skin on the back of her hands. "'Tis not your nightmares that hold you back?"

"Nay, I do not believe so. I have conquered my fears there, yet something deep inside me tells me to stay here."

"I think you should go. This is a chance you may never get again. What is one sennight or fortnight when you could have regrets the rest of your life?"

His voice sounded thick with exhaustion, so she climbed back out of bed and kissed him. "Aye, you are right. If you promise me not to fall in love with another while I'm away, then I will go."

"I promise. My heart is in your hands, and we will wait for you."

As if on cue, Mada looked up at her and gave a short bark.

"You see, Mada and Sim agree."

"I must give my answer to Uncle Logan, and then tell my mother and stepsire."

When Magnus told her he loved her this time, it felt like a promise. Her heart was completely lost to him, and she prayed he would guard it well.

The following morn, Ashlyn delivered her instructions to the men after first discussing her plan with Uncle Logan. The men had contained their surprise well when Uncle Logan had announced she would be in charge of the group of warriors heading to Edinburgh. Of course, they had all heard about Ashlyn's feats on the first mission.

A moon ago, she would have been bursting with pride at this change, but a wee voice in the back of her mind continued to niggle at her, urging her to stay. She hadn't slept well, but she hadn't had the usual nightmares either.

The snow had mostly melted, probably making room for more, as the saying went. She'd said a few prayers last night that she'd get back to Grant land before the heavy snows fell. As they rode out, many of the clan's young lads and lassies followed them toward the Grant border, running and yelling and cheering.

One lass with long, dark hair stayed beside her for as long as she could. Ashlyn waved at the lass, and they smiled at each other. When the lass finally tired, she slowed her steps but yelled after her, "Promise you'll come back, my lady? You belong here, do you not? You'll not go back to your home when you were young, will you?"

A few more horse lengths, and the voice still carried to her. "Promise to come back?"

She jerked her head around as a memory stole over, so vivid it brought her back to a forgotten moment in time.

She was back in Ayr near the beach. She and Gracie sat on a rock, Gracie's head in her lap. Her wee sister was crying because her mother's boyfriend had yelled at the two of them to leave. Ashlyn had tugged on Gracie and pulled her outside while their mother argued with the cruel lad.

She brushed the white curls back from Gracie's face, then leaned down to whisper to her. "Gracie, mayhap someday Mama will find another. And he'll take us far, far away from here. We'll have a new home, one with a big hearth in it, and a fire every night to keep us warm." She moved her hand to Gracie's back, softly rubbing her skin under the coarse cloth of her gown, doing her best to calm the wee lassie. "Mama will cook for us every night, and we'll help her chop the vegetables and throw them into the pot on the hearth. We shall never go hungry again. Mayhap they will marry, and her new husband will love us and always be kind, and he'll have brothers and sisters so we'll have a big family full of aunts and uncles." Oh, how she wished it could be true.

Gracie, who rarely spoke, sat up and gazed into her eyes and whispered one word, "Promise?"

Ashlyn had kissed her wee sister's cheek and replied, "If we ever find a home like that, I promise we'll never have to leave."

*Promise.* The very same word Gracie had said to her when they'd discussed her marrying Magnus. This was the memory that still haunted her, not the nightmares. How fortunate they were to have come to Clan Grant. She remembered her words and her feelings as though it had just happened.

A lump in her throat kept her from speaking, but once she was able to control it, she steered her horse over to Aunt Gwyneth's mount. "I'm sorry, Aunt Gwyneth. I do not wish to disappoint you. You know how much I love you and appreciate all you've done for me and Gracie, but I cannot do this. This is not me." She turned to Uncle Logan and said, "I must go back. Forgive me, but I do not belong here. I belong on Grant land with my family and with Magnus."

Uncle Logan smiled and nodded. "We wondered how long it would be before you figured that out for yourself, lass."

"Ashlyn, you could never disappoint us by making the choice that's right for you. You must trust your instincts. That much we've both taught you. You've had a most difficult life," Aunt Gwyneth said, "and you deserve happiness. Now go find him." She winked at her and waved her off.

Ashlyn turned her horse around and headed back to the castle, tears running down her face as she made peace with her decision and her new life. Aye, Gracie and her family would still be a major part of her life, but she had room for one more.

Magnus. And it was time she told him.

Once she reached the top of the hill, she jumped off her horse. Magnus sat on a rock throwing sticks for his dogs, a huge smile on his face. Her heart lodged in her throat at the sight of him. She yelled his name, and he turned to wave to her.

So full of emotion she could not speak, Ashlyn raced down the hill and threw herself into his arms. "Your fever is gone already? Should you not be inside?"

"Not completely gone yet, but I feel much better, and the dogs were anxious to retrieve their sticks. Your mother's potions and poultices have helped quite a bit. What is it? You have a strange look on your face. I thought you were going to Edinburgh. Did I miss something?"

When she was finally able to keep her tears in check, she kissed him, devouring him.

Many moments later, she finally pulled back, and he grinned at her—that wonderful grin he almost always wore, but this one had a quirk to it that seemed to be just for her. "I love you, Magnus, and if you'll still have me, naught would make me happier than to be your wife."

"I love you, too, and you have no idea how much your words please me, Ashlyn. But you changed your mind? You are not going to Edinburgh?"

She shook her head with such certainty she surprised herself. "Nay. I'd prefer to stay here with you. You and I belong together, right here on Grant land. I wish to look forward, not backward."

He cupped her cheeks and kissed her softly, and she had to fight to keep from crying because something happened inside her that she had thought would never, ever happen in her lifetime.

Her heart sang.

# EPILOGUE

*One year later*

Ashlyn paced the front chamber, her hands massaging her swollen belly, taking deep breaths to try to calm the pain rippling through her body. When the contraction ended, she moved over to her husband, the fear on his face so evident that it broke her heart. He was so agitated he leaned against the wall instead of sitting.

She knew what was going on in his head. He was reliving that fateful night when his wee wife Rhona had died giving birth to the son who had died along with her. Magnus had been left alone with a broken heart. His losses had almost crushed him.

She stood on the tips of her toes, cupped his cheek, and kissed him. "Magnus, I wish I could give you a potion to make you sleep until this was over. Then you would not have to go through such hell."

"Nay. No potion. Just promise me."

"I will be here, I promise. We will raise this bairn together."

The sweat beaded on his forehead and he dried it with a linen square. "I have a favor to ask, 'tis quite unusual."

A knock on the door interrupted them. "Enter." Ashlyn hollered.

Her mother flew in the door with Gracie behind her. Caralyn glanced at her daughter first and then at Magnus. "Oh, Magnus. While I cannot promise, I think this will be much different for you. Maddie is coming to help. Why do you not go visit with Robbie while she brings your bairn into the world?"

Magnus shook his head, not taking his gaze off his wife for an instant.

"Mama, I'm fine. I just finished a pain, and Magnus was telling me he had a special request. Go ahead and finish. Whatever it is, we shall do it if it will ease your mind."

He swallowed before he spoke and took her hand in his. "I wish to stay by your side. I know Alex sat behind Maddie whenever she delivered, but I do not wish to be behind you. I must be able to look at you."

"Why, Magnus?" Ashlyn had been at many births, so she knew it was an unusual request. He was going to have a difficult time until the bairn was here and in her arms awake and well. "Do you know how horrible I shall look, or how loud I may get?"

Caralyn arranged all her tools on the table, handing the bucket to Gracie to go for water. "Magnus, 'tis her first. It could be a verra long time for her. You'll fall off the stool."

"Nay, I will not. I will be able to handle aught so long as I can see her."

"But why? There is naught you can do." Ashlyn stood next to him and rested her head on his shoulder. She was afraid she would frighten him if she yelled or screamed, and she did not want to upset him more.

"Aye, there is." His voice shook as he spoke, telling her how emotional he was at this moment.

"What?"

Ashlyn and her mother stood in front of him, awaiting his answer.

"If you do die, I can tell you I love you and hold you while you pass. I could not do that with Rhona. Please. I wish to stay by your side, mayhap I can help you."

"Of course," Ashlyn whispered, barely able to get a sound past the catch in her throat. When she was able, she said, "I would love to have you by my side."

"Why not?" Caralyn agreed. "I am willing to try something new. Please do me a favor and find a chair instead of a stool. I heard Kyle Maule fell right off the back of his stool when he saw his twins."

A few hours later, Ashlyn pushed, cursing at everything in sight but her husband. She swore this bairn would never come out of her. She heaved and grunted, her husband gripping her hand, his eyes never leaving her as she labored to deliver their firstborn.

He'd stayed by her side, never wavering, kissing her, whispering soft words to her as she bellowed to the mighty trees above.

"Come, Ashlyn, push! The bairn is almost out. One strong push should do it. I see dark hair," her mother said. She and Aunt Maddie had been whispering encouragements throughout the birthing. Gracie stood opposite Magnus, at turns mopping Ashlyn's forehead and holding her other hand.

Tears blurred Ashlyn's vision as she fought her frustration and exhaustion and pushed with all her might. The bairn finally slid out of her and landed in her mother's arms. She fell back on the pillows, panting from exertion, and closed her eyes as her huge sigh of relief echoed through the chamber.

Magnus jumped up from his chair as soon as her eyes closed. "Ashlyn, you promised me. You will not die on me."

Her eyes flew open. "I'm not dying, husband. I just needed a moment's rest. 'Twas hard work." She cupped his cheek with her hand, and he leaned down to kiss her on the mouth.

Then it dawned on her. "What is it, Mama? A lad or a lassie?"

"Congratulations! You have a beautiful lassie." As if on cue, their daughter let out a wail, screaming loud enough to wake everyone in the land, her hands fisted and swinging.

"And a strong lassie. Listen to that voice." Aunt Maddie leaned over to kiss Ashlyn's cheek before she moved back to help clean the wee bairn before bundling her.

Ashlyn peered at her husband, and his head fell forward as if in prayer, so she said naught, giving him this time for himself. When he lifted his head, she was shocked at the contortion on his face. "Magnus, are you not happy with a lass?" He'd never let on that he wished for a son. Then her big, strapping husband suddenly did something that she would never have expected.

Magnus burst into tears. When he had calmed down a wee bit, he lifted her so he could sit on the bed and settle her on his lap. Wrapping his arms around her, he cried into her shoulder. Her mother finished cleaning the bairn and placed the wee bundle in Ashlyn's arms and then kissed her daughter's cheek before stepping back.

Ashlyn's husband, tears covering his face, managed to say, "She's just what I'd prayed for, a wee lassie, strong like her mama."

# NOVELS BY KEIRA MONTCLAIR

# DEAR READERS,

I hope you enjoyed my fifth novel in THE HIGHLAND CLAN series, *Ashlyn*. If you are interested in learning more about Ashlyn's younger days, Robbie and Caralyn's story was told in *Journey to the Highlands*, the fourth in the Clan Grant series. Molly's story is next, and I am excited to tell her story.

If you want to know more about my novels, here are some places for you to visit.

1. Visit my website at www.keiramontclair.com and sign up for my newsletter. I'll keep you updated about my new releases without bothering you often.

2. **Go to my Facebook page and 'like' me:** You will get updates on any new novels, book signings, and giveaways. https://www.facebook.com/KeiraMontclair

3. **Stop by my Pinterest page:** http://www.pinterest.com/KeiraMontclair/ You'll see how I envision Ashlyn and Magnus.

4. **Leave a review on Amazon or Goodreads.** Reviews help self-published authors like me and help other readers as well.

**Continue on for an excerpt from *Journey to the Highlands*, the story of Robbie, Caralyn, Ashlyn, and Gracie.**

Happy reading!
Keira Montclair
www.keiramontclair.com

# ABOUT THE AUTHOR

Keira Montclair is the pen name of an author who lives in Florida with her husband. She loves to write fast-paced, emotional romance, especially with children as secondary characters in her stories.

She has worked as a registered nurse in pediatrics and recovery room nursing. Teaching is another of her loves, and she has taught both high school mathematics and practical nursing.

Now she loves to spend her time writing, but there isn't enough time to write everything she wants! Her Highlander Clan Grant series, comprising of eight standalone novels, is a reader favorite. Her third series, The Highland Clan, set twenty years after the Clan Grant series, focuses on the Grant/Ramsay descendants. She also has a contemporary series set in The Finger Lakes of Western New York.

You may contact her through her website at www.keiramontclair.com. She also has a Facebook account and a twitter account through Keira Montclair. If you send her an email through her website, she promises to respond.

# AN EXCERPT FROM:

# JOURNEY TO THE HIGHLANDS

## CHAPTER ONE

*1263, Autumn*
*Ayrshire, Scotland*

Caralyn of the Crauford House stilled, shushing her lass of eight summers to silence with a swish of her hand. Laughter echoed across the land—not the happy sound so loved by her clan, but the ribald guffaws of invaders hell-bent on doing their worst. That sound inched up the back of her neck, raising the hairs there.

*Norsemen.* Rumors of the pillaging already done by the men on those Norse galley ships had spread through the small coastal villages of Scotland like wildfire, but she had hoped they would somehow miss her small fishing village, tucked away at the edge of her clan. Caralyn peeked out through the fur coverings across her window and saw her worst nightmare—men with torches running up the paths between cottages, hollering in a foreign tongue.

Caralyn whirled to face her daughter and whispered, "Ashlyn, get your sister."

They tore through the two room cottage for the wee lassie, her beloved wean. "Gracie? Gracie, where are you?" As they stepped into the bed chamber, her blonde haired, blue-eyed daughter waddled toward her, her arms raised in the usual manner to entice her mama to lift her up. At just over two summers, she spoke little, but understood everything.

Caralyn picked Gracie up and moved toward the back door. "Get the sack, Ashlyn."

They had been warned the Norse could come. King Haakon of Norway, furious at the actions of the Scottish King Alexander III, had sailed up the Firth of Clyde. Rumor had said the enemies were headed to the royal burgh at Ayr, but given the number of longboats and galleys anchored off Arran, they could stop anywhere along the way. Men at war could be ruthless; that much she knew, especially after the tales she had heard about their plundering in other seaside villages. The raven banners of Haakon's fleet had already been seen off Kintyre, where his men had ravaged the mainland.

Why had Malcolm taken her guards with him the other day? Now they were completely without protection. Caralyn had done what she could to prepare, forcing her daughters to practice hiding over and over. Simply put, the Norsemen would have to kill her first before they touched her lassies.

Ashlyn appeared around the corner, tying the small sack to her waist. "Mama, come with us?"

Caralyn put her fingers to her daughter's lips. "Shush, love. I will follow as soon as I can. Now do as we practiced. Take your sister and run until you find the rocks, then hide. Do not come out for any reason. I will find you."

The look of terror in her daughter's eyes wrenched her gut. Someday, she vowed she would eliminate the fear in Ashlyn's eyes, but today, she had no choice but to send them ahead without her. She knew what she had to do to protect her bairns. If she were to go with the girls, the Norseman would follow them. Caralyn would draw the attackers away and distract them; she knew what they wanted.

Caralyn knelt and kissed both girls. "Promise Mama. Do you hear me, Ashlyn? Mama could not bear to have anything happen to her sweet lassies." She pushed them out the back door and followed behind them. "Go."

As soon as she stepped outdoors, her ears rang from a sharp war whoop. She turned to see a large man with a flaming torch race for her cottage. Only a few had made it this far, but her home could be brought down with a single torch. He touched the edge to the corner of the roof and the thatch roared to life, burning and smoking in a fury.

The man's gaze caught hers and he grinned before he yelled in exultation, throwing his torch in the dirt and beating his chest as if she were a glorious prize. Aye, she knew what he wanted. She yelled, "Run, Ashlyn. Run!"

Caralyn took off in the opposite direction, hoping she'd caught his attention enough for him to leave the girls and follow her. Out of the corner of her eye, she noticed Ashlyn running toward the beach as they had planned. Caralyn fingered her dagger in the folds of the pocket she had sewn into her skirts. A last resort. *Lord, help me be strong, I will fight. I will fight for my girls. Please help me.*

Her boots carried her down the path toward the center of the village where the fishermen kept their boats. Was anyone around to help? She glanced over her shoulder and noticed the Norseman had fallen for her plan and chased after her, his long strides bringing him closer every instant. Peeking to her right, she thanked God that her girls could no longer be seen and she prayed they were safe. Ashlyn was a strong lass, as she had been forced to be. The Lord would keep them in his hands.

A large paw grabbed her hair and wrenched her backward. She landed with a grunt and her assailant chuckled. The raw odor of filthy flesh assaulted her nostrils as she glanced up to see the smile on his dirt-encrusted face. She recognized that look. It was an expression of sheer, perverse desire; this man hadn't been with a woman for so long that sexual need fueled his every move. He craved her body for what it was, a means to an end, with flagrant disregard for her soul and her emotions. Licking the side of her face, he palmed her breast through her wool gown. He was no different than any other man. He wouldn't stop until he raped her.

So be it. He could do as he wished with her as long as he stayed away from her lassies. She would do anything to guarantee their safety. Rape her, beat her, she could handle anything as long as he didn't touch her daughters.

One meaty hand clutched a death grip on her arm, and he pulled her up and turned to the side of the path as if looking for a spot to bed her. But he stilled, listening to his surroundings, glancing all around. She guessed he looked for his comrades, but none were visible.

As if having made a decision, he yanked her arm and tugged her behind him toward the coastline. She struggled to keep up as he took an alternate route through a thick group of trees. What in hell was he planning? Caralyn had been able to calm herself when she'd expected to be thrown into the bushes and forced to submit to him. She dreaded his touch, but she understood such a fate. She could handle it. Now she swallowed in an attempt to slow her pounding heart because she had no idea where they were going. The unknown frightened her and she knew not what he was about. His demeanor had transformed, subtly, but enough for her to know his goal had changed. As soon as they broke through the trees onto the vast shoreline, he yelled down the beach to his friends. Caralyn stumbled along beside him, but froze when her gaze settled on their destination, realization smacking her hard between the eyes.

A longboat. He was dragging her to his ship. He wanted to take her on his galley to service all his comrades, too. Not another female was in sight, though she saw one unmoving clump of wool not far away. A shock of hair stuck out from the pile. Who was it, someone she knew? Was she already dead? *Calm yourself, Caralyn, you can beat them, but only if you are in control.* She forced several deep breaths into her lungs, willing herself to relax.

But she couldn't. A longboat, he was taking her to the longboat, and he would tear her away from her girls. And what would become of her once she stepped onto that ship? They would use her as they saw fit, then toss her overboard. She could swim, but not from the center of the firth.

Never. Never would he get her onto that ship. She had to think and act quickly. She thought of her girls, of Gracie's big blue eyes staring at her. Who would care for them if something happened to her? They were her life, quite simply. The only thing she valued in this entire world sat hidden between rocks down the beach. Even though she hadn't been able to provide the best of lives for them, she was determined to change that if she survived this ordeal.

Unleashing the pent up anger for all the injustices she had been dealt, she corralled that fury, directing it toward this one man in front of her. The foreigners could beat her, have their way with her, but she was not leaving her daughters, not now, not ever. They were still quite a distance from the ship, enough for her to fight and get away. And fight she would.

Caralyn screamed and grabbed her dagger from her hidden pocket, sinking it into the brute's thigh. He bellowed and let go of her arm for an instant, just enough time for her to dart away. She scurried back toward the path, but didn't make it far before he grabbed her plaited hair, swung her around, and slapped her.

Cheers went up from the galley ship, but no one came to the

man's aid, thankfully. This would be a performance for his shipmates to watch. The lass against the Norseman, and she would fight with everything she had.

"You vile brute, leave me be!" She screamed and clawed, spit and bit. He hit her in the belly, but the pain didn't sway her. When he looked away from her for a moment to remove the dagger from his thigh, she kicked him in the groin and he crumpled to the ground, losing the knife in the sand. Hoots from the galleys continued. Pivoting, she tried to run, but he grabbed her ankle and she toppled face down into the gravel. He pulled her back slowly toward him, running his hand over her bare leg under her skirts. She flipped onto her back and kicked him in the jaw with her other foot.

He cursed and released her.

Caralyn searched for her dagger in the sand, but didn't see it. The lout managed to get to his feet and swayed over her. Pushing herself upright, she grabbed the biggest rock she could find and swung it straight at his head. When she connected with his temple and a resounding thud rang out in the air, she hoped he would fall, but instead he stared at her, a low growl tearing through his throat and settling into a furious expression. He picked her up by both arms and tossed her in the air. Unable to catch her fall, she hit the ground at an odd angle, twisting her ankle under her. She screamed in pain as she landed in the dirt. He jumped on top of her, pulled his fist back, set to demolish her face, and the last thing she recalled before darkness enveloped her was Gracie's sad eyes.

*Journey to the Highlands* is available in digital form, print, and audio.

www.ingramcontent.com/pod-product-compliance
Lightning Source LLC
Chambersburg PA
CBHW060938180626
46817CB00004B/1612